Simply Learning, Simply Best!

Simply Learning, Simply Best!

倍斯特出版事業有限公司
Best Publishing Ltd.

我的第一本
動畫故事
親子英語

郭玥慧 ◎ 著

MP3

以小朋友最愛的動畫為主題開口說英文
用一部部動畫電影輕鬆學英文閱讀和口說

這本書讓動畫電影成為最棒的親子英文教材！

- **精選36篇動畫故事**，這一次不只看動畫，讀有趣的英文動畫，學英文也細細品嚐它們帶給孩子和爸媽的**感動和小道理**。

- **基礎篇和進階篇**──帶著孩子從短文章開始，從**150字初階文章**後進階到**250字的長文章**，適合**8-16歲的孩子**！

- **MP3光碟聽讀OK**──MP3是親子共讀的好幫手，親子跟著MP3**一起讀**或讓孩子**自己聽**故事！

陪伴您的孩子使用英語，變成更好的人。

　　動畫不止是娛樂來源，更是學習的好工具。這本書以英語動畫為出發點，用心提供一些可以切入的主題，親子可以透過輕鬆的影片討論較嚴肅的主題，一同面對或反省一些問題。其次，我將整部或部分動畫濃縮為較簡單的短文，除了讓孩子可以透過閱讀，學習到更多英語字句之外，也讓孩子間接累積彙整與表達的能力。年紀較大或程度較好的孩子如果能在看完影片與文章之後，用自己的話或是模仿文章描述劇情，將會是非常好的訓練。

　　更重要的是，我希望孩子能瞭解到，語言是項工具，而不只是一門科目。語言能讓你更快取得資訊，你能透過語言學習並與人討論很多事情 ，因此在書中也加入了相關主題可以使用的一些句子。

　　希望這本書能讓孩子在英語以及想法都有所提升。

郭玥慧老師

EDITOR 編者序

　　幼兒時期練習口說是最佳的時機，孩子們不會害怕犯錯或是害羞而不敢開口，講久了自然成習慣。家長們都希望把握這個黃金學習時機，讓自己的孩子早早說出一口道地的英語，但畢竟爸媽們也不是英語學習專家，該怎麼教小朋友說英文呢？現在就帶著你的孩子從閱讀動畫故事開始，練習英語會話吧！

　　想要練習英文會話時，建議從你最感興趣的話題開始吧！許多親子英語學習書籍都以常見的日常生活句子為學習主題，那如果小朋友想要用英文表達自己的看法呢？從小朋友最愛的卡通下手吧！動畫是專屬小朋友的電影，色彩繽紛又立體的動畫人物躍上大螢幕，甚至連大人都會忍不住愛上呢！動畫的主題包羅萬象，有學校、親子相處、成長、友誼和追求夢想，這都是和小朋友討論的口說好主題。動畫電影用討喜的卡通人物向小小孩解釋這個世界，因此動畫故事也是最好的教養教材。

　　本書單元設計從閱讀大小朋友熟悉且喜愛的動畫故事開始—「主題小劇場」，讀完故事，認識單字，「一句一句練習說」進一步開口說一說與動畫電影相關的會話主題，簡單的句型讓大人小孩一起學習不費力！

　　此外，特別設計「帶著寶貝一起讀」介紹屬於每一部動畫的教養小提醒，讓爸媽帶著孩子在閱讀故事前更容易融入劇情，鼓勵爸媽帶著孩子一起討論劇情，從劇情中好好品嘗動畫帶給我們的感動，謝謝玥慧老師透過動畫電影寫出這麼棒且適合親子共讀的小故事，希望藉著這些小故事，讓爸媽和小朋友都愛上學英文，也享受難得且美好的親子時光。

倍斯特編輯部

目錄
CONTENTS

1 Part
Basic 基礎篇

2 Part • • •
Let's Learn More 更上一層樓

使用說明
INSTRUCTIONS

 帶著寶貝一起讀

爸媽該如何帶小朋友看這一部動畫呢？這邊給爸媽每一部動畫的教養小重點，可以帶著小朋友這樣看動畫。讀讀英文故事前，先跟孩子談一談，讓他們更能融入劇情唷！

Unit 1 怪獸電力公司 Monsters, Inc.
A laugh is more powerful
歡笑的力量更強大

帶著寶貝一起讀

有時我們在面對人與人之間的問題，會馬上生氣、用威嚇的方式，快速的解決問題。 但這樣，有時反而讓問題變得更嚴重。 有時不需要一直逃避或委屈自己，其實面對衝突，還有許多更適合的解決方法，像是堅定但友善地說出自己的感受，或是退一步一同分享一個東西。 相信你很快也會跟毛怪 Sulley 一樣，發現歡笑與愛比生氣與恨的力量大多了。 想想有什麼其他好方法吧！

Parents   Grandparents

主題小劇場 MP3 001 ▶

In the city of Monstropolis, some monsters work in the power company, Monsters, Inc. They provide energy for the city by going into children's rooms through the children's closet doors to collect their screams. This is why they are called scarers. One day, a little girl named Boo accidentally enters the monster world. Sulley the monster, along with his friend, Mike, tries to bring Boo back to her bedroom.

While Boo is with them, the two monsters find out that making kids laugh actually produces even more power than scaring kids. Sometime later, Sulley becomes the new CEO of the power company. The monsters in the power company stop scaring children to power their city. Instead, they go into children's rooms to make them laugh.

017

主題小劇場

用英文讀一讀有趣的動畫情節，是否又勾起小朋友和爸媽的回憶呢？
帶著孩子一起讀，親子共讀英文增添更多趣味。

我的第一本動畫親子英語

在怪獸城市裡面，有些怪獸在怪獸電力公司裡面工作。這些怪獸從小孩的衣櫃進到房間裡面，來收集小孩的尖叫，幫城市發電，所以他們被稱為「驚嚇員」。有一天，小女孩阿布（Boo）不小心闖進了怪獸的世界，毛怪（Sulley）和他的朋友大眼仔（Mike）試圖要帶阿布回她的房間。

阿布在身邊的這段時間，毛怪和大眼仔發現，原來小孩大笑產生的電力比驚嚇小孩來的更強大。不久之後，毛怪成了電力公司的老闆，相反的是怪獸不再嚇小孩，他們改讓孩子大笑。

018

兩大篇：初階篇和進階篇

分為初階篇和進階篇，每一篇初階文章不超過 300 字；讀完初階後，更上一層樓，挑戰看看每一篇 500 字的進階篇。搭配中文譯文和 MP3 一起唸英文更簡單！

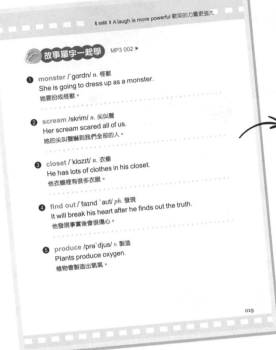

故事單字一起學　MP3 002 ▶

1 monster /ˈgɑrdn/ *n.* 怪獸
She is going to dress up as a monster.
她要扮成怪獸。

2 scream /skrim/ *n.* 尖叫聲
Her scream scared all of us.
她的尖叫聲嚇到我們全部的人。

3 closet /ˈklɑzɪt/ *n.* 衣櫥
He has lots of clothes in his closet.
他衣櫥裡有很多衣服。

4 find out /faɪnd ˈaut/ *ph.* 發現
It will break his heart after he finds out the truth.
他發現事實後會很傷心。

5 produce /prəˈdjus/ *v.* 製造
Plants produce oxygen.
植物會製造出氧氣。

019

MP3音檔學習

從「主題小劇場」到「主題單字心智圖」皆附錄音，帶著孩子跟著 CD 一起唸，英文卡卡也不怕，邊聽邊練習唸出正確發音。

故事單字一起學

讀完文章馬上學文章中的單字，印象最深刻也學得快！

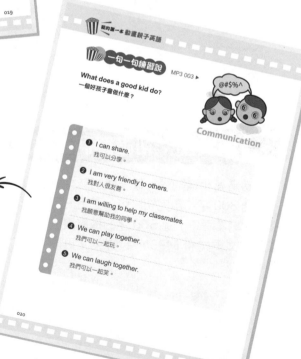

我的第一本 動畫親子英語

一句一句練習說　MP3 003 ▶

What does a good kid do?
一個好孩子會做什麼？

@#$%^

Communication

1 I can share.
我可以分享。

2 I am very friendly to others.
我對人很友善。

3 I am willing to help my classmates.
我願意幫助我的同學。

4 We can play together.
我們可以一起玩。

5 We can laugh together.
我們可以一起笑。

020

一句一句練習說

用相關主題帶著孩子練習說，難易適中的短句和貼近生活的句子，一問多答實用百分百！

主題單字心智圖　　MP3 004 ▶

classmate /ˈklɑːsˌmeɪt/ *n.* 同學
Sarah is the smartest student of my classmates.
莎拉是我同學中最聰明的一位。

together /təˈgeðə(r)/ *adj.* 一起的
I always do my homework together with my classmates.
我總是和我的同學一起寫功課。

share /ʃɛr/ *v.* 分享
We can share this toy.
我們可以一起玩這個玩具。

laugh /læf/ *v.* 笑
I like her because she makes me laugh.
我喜歡她，她總是可以讓我笑。

friendly /ˈfren(d)li/ *adj.* 友善的、善良的
I enjoy working there – everyone is so friendly.
我喜歡在這裡工作，每一個同事都很友善。

主題單字心智圖

主題圖案增加背單字的趣味性，主題圖
案為記憶單字增加趣味，減少記憶單字
的負擔。

PART **1**

BASIC

基礎篇

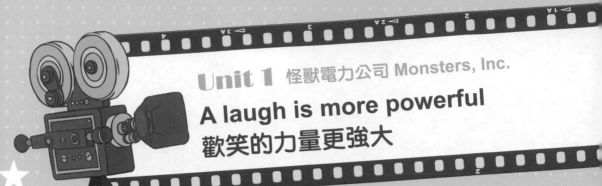

Unit 1 怪獸電力公司 Monsters, Inc.

A laugh is more powerful
歡笑的力量更強大

帶著寶貝一起讀

　　有時我們在面對人與人之間的問題，會馬上生氣、用威嚇的方式，快速的解決問題。 但這樣，有時反而讓問題變得更嚴重。 有時不需要一直逃避或委屈自己，其實面對衝突，還有許多更適合的解決方法，像是堅定但友善地說出自己的感受，或是退一步一同分享一個東西。 相信你很快也會跟毛怪 Sulley 一樣，發現歡笑與愛比生氣與恨的力量大多了。想想有什麼其他好方法吧！

Parents

Grandparents

 MP3 001 ▶

In the city of Monstropolis, some **monster**s work in the power company, Monsters, Inc. They provide energy for the city by going into children's rooms through the children's **closet** doors to collect their **scream**s. This is why they are called scarers. One day, a little girl named Boo accidentally enters the monster world. Sulley the monster, along with his friend, Mike, tries to bring Boo back to her bedroom.

While Boo is with them, the two monsters **find out** that making kids laugh actually **produce**s even more power than scaring kids. Sometime later, Sulley becomes the new CEO of the power company. The monsters in the power company stop scaring children to power their city. Instead, they go into children's rooms to make them laugh.

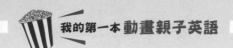

在怪獸城市裡面，有些怪獸在怪獸電力公司裡面工作。這些怪獸會從小孩的衣櫃進到房間裡面，來收集小孩的尖叫，幫城市發電，所以他們被稱為「驚嚇員」。有一天，小女孩阿布（Boo）不小心闖進了怪獸的世界，毛怪（Sulley）和他的朋友大眼仔（Mike）試圖要帶阿布回她的房間。

阿布在身邊的這段時間，毛怪和大眼仔發現，原來小孩大笑產生的電力比驚嚇小孩來的更強大。不久之後，毛怪成了電力公司的老闆，相反的是怪獸不再嚇小孩，牠們改讓孩子大笑。

故事單字一起學 MP3 002 ▶

❶ monster /ˈmɑːn.stɚ/ *n.* 怪獸
She is going to dress up as a monster.
她要扮成怪獸。

❷ scream /skrim/ *n.* 尖叫聲
Her scream scared all of us.
她的尖叫聲嚇到我們全部的人。

❸ closet /ˈklɑzɪt/ *n.* 衣櫥
He has lots of clothes in his closet.
他衣櫥裡有很多衣服。

❹ find out /ˈfaɪnd ˈaʊt/ *ph.* 發現
It will break his heart after he finds out the truth.
他發現事實後會很傷心。

❺ produce /prəˈdjus/ *v.* 製造
Plants produce oxygen.
植物會製造出氧氣。

一句一句練習說　MP3 003 ▶

@#$%^

What does a good kid do?
一個好孩子會做什麼？

Communication

❶ I can share.
我可以分享。

❷ I am very friendly to others.
我對人很友善。

❸ I am willing to help my classmates.
我願意幫助我的同學。

❹ We can play together.
我們可以一起玩。

❺ We can laugh together.
我們可以一起笑。

 主題單字心智圖　MP3 004 ▶

classmate /ˈklɑːsˌmeɪt/ **n.** 同學

Sarah is the smartest student of my classmates.
莎拉是我同學中最聰明的一位。

together /təˈgeðə(r)/ **adj.** 一起的

I always do my homework together with my classmates.
我總是和我的同學一起寫功課。

share /ʃɛr/ **v.** 分享

We can share this toy.
我們可以一起玩這個玩具。

laugh /læf/ **v.** 笑

I like her because she makes me laugh.
我喜歡她，她總是可以讓我笑。

friendly/ˈfren(d)li/ **adj.** 友善的、善良的

I enjoy working there – everyone is so friendly.
我喜歡在這裡工作，每一個同事都很友善。

Unit 2 怪獸電力公司 Monsters, Inc.
Face Your Fears
面對你的恐懼

帶著寶貝一起讀

　　人生總會遇到許多我們害怕、不敢做的事。而我們總會因為恐懼，選擇逃避。但這樣的恐懼會讓我們錯過許多事物。很多時候，這些恐懼都只在我們腦中，我們把事情想的很恐怖，而且這個恐懼可能不斷被放大，我們把它越想越嚴重。如果我們實際去面對這些恐懼就會發現，這些事物並沒有我們想像的恐怖。就像電影裡面的怪獸一樣，以為小孩很恐怖，相處之後發現小孩根本無害。想想有哪些事情是你不敢嘗試的，你願不願意試試看呢？

Parents

Grandparents

 MP3 005 ▶

The monster, George, **finish**es one of his routine scares and walks back through a door. When he turns around, a **child**'s white sock can be seen on his back. Suddenly, the **alarm** sounds and sends the floor into a panic. George screams for people to get the sock off. The Child Detection Agency rushes to the scene to destroy the sock and shave off George's hair. This is how much monsters are afraid of children.

When Sulley the monster first sees the girl, Boo, in the monster world, he is really scared. He can't even touch the girl. After spending some time with the girl, Sulley grows attached to her and **realize**s that human children are not as deadly as **rumor**ed.

　　怪獸喬治（George）結束他的例行驚嚇工作，穿過門走了回來，當他轉過來的時候，在他的背上看到了一隻小孩的白色襪子。警鈴突然響起，整層樓陷入驚慌，喬治尖叫，要人把襪子拿下來。「兒童探測局」衝到現場，把襪子摧毀，然後把喬治的毛剃光。從這幕可以看出怪獸們有多害怕小孩。

　　當毛怪（Sulley）第一次在怪獸的世界裡看到小女孩阿布（Boo）的時候，也是非常的恐懼，他連碰都不敢碰。在和阿布相處一段時間之後，毛怪越來越喜歡阿布，而且發現其實小孩不像流傳的那樣致命。

 故事單字一起學　MP3 006 ▶

❶ finish /ˈfɪnɪʃ/ *v.* 完成
When can you finish your homework?
你什麼時候可以完成作業？

❷ child /tʃaɪld/ *n.* 小孩
I'm the youngest child in my family.
我是家裏最小的小孩。

❸ alarm /əˈlɑrm/ *n.* 警報
The fire alarm went off at school today.
今天在學校火災警報發生。

❹ realize /ˈrɪəˌlaɪz/ *v.* 了解
I realize that I can be great.
我了解到我可以變得偉大。

❺ rumor /ˈwɔtɚ/ *v.* 謠傳
It is rumored that he bought an island.
傳言說他買了一座小島。

一句一句練習說　MP3 007 ▶

@#$%^

What are you afraid of?
你害怕什麼東西？

Communication

❶ I do not like cats.
我不喜歡貓。

❷ I am afraid of the water.
我怕水。

❸ I'm afraid of bugs.
我怕蟲。

❹ I'm afraid of the darkness.
我怕黑。

❺ I'm afraid of ghosts.
我怕鬼。

 主題單字心智圖　MP3 008 ▶

water /ˋwɔtɚ/ *n.* 水

I like to play in the water.
我喜歡在水裡玩。

ghost /gost/ *n.* 鬼魂

He told me a ghost story.
他說了一個鬼故事。

afraid /əˋfred/ *adj.* 害怕的

I am afraid of dogs.
我怕狗。

bug /bʌg/ *n.* 蟲子

There are so many bugs in the bathroom.
廁所好多蟲子喔。

in the dark *ph.* 在黑暗中

I cannot see clearly in the dark.
我在黑暗中看不清楚。

Unit 3 冰雪奇緣 Frozen

Accept your true self
擁抱真實的自己

🎬 帶著寶貝一起讀

　　你和兄弟姊妹或是朋友同學有什麼不同的地方嗎？你擔心自己這些跟別人不一樣的地方？人常常害怕展現真正的自己，例如不敢讓同學知道我們真正喜歡或想做的事，因為擔心別人的眼光。電影中艾莎刻意遠離人群，總是自己一個人來隱藏與別人的不同。因此艾莎一直沒有機會學習面對自己的魔法，在日後反而不小心造成更大的傷害。當我們隱藏自己的時候，我們都忘記這些不同之處才是最珍貴的禮物，讓每個人都可以成為獨特的自己。所以不要擔心！正向面對你的不同，並好好發揮它吧！

Parents

Grandparents

Elsa, the **Princess** of Arendelle, is **born** with **special** ice powers. When she was a kid, her younger sister, Anna, enjoyed playing with Elsa because Elsa could create an ice playground and make snow right in the castle. While they were playing one morning, Elsa accidentally injured Anna with her magic powers. After that, Elsa conceals her powers and grows up away from people, including her sister.

On the day that Elsa becomes Queen, she unleashes her powers by **accident**. This brings a forever winter to Arendelle because she has not learned how to control her powers. Elsa has no choice but flees the castle. Anna follows to bring her sister back. After some struggles, and with Anna's and friends' support, Elsa knows how to **control** her powers and is able to use her magic to bring happiness to people around her now.

　　艾倫戴爾（Arendelle）的公主艾莎（Elsa）出生時就擁有神奇的冰雪魔法。因為艾莎可以在城堡裡變出雪和冰雪遊樂場，所以她的妹妹安娜（Anna）很喜歡和艾莎玩。有一天早上，兩個女孩在玩耍時，艾莎的魔法不小心傷到了安娜。從此之後，艾莎再也不展現她的魔法，並刻意不與人往來，和妹妹也不再一起玩。

　　在艾莎成為皇后的那天，艾莎不小心釋出她的魔法。因為艾莎從沒學會控制她的魔法，這不小心把艾倫戴爾帶進永恆的冬天。慌張之下，艾莎逃離城堡，安娜出發想帶回艾莎。歷經曲折之後，在安娜和朋友的支持下，艾莎知道如何控制自己的魔法，還能透過魔法帶給人們快樂。

 MP3 010 ▶

❶ **princess** /ˋprɪnsɪs/ *n.* 公主
His daughter is his princess.
他的女兒是他的小公主。

. . . .

❷ **born** /bɔrn/ *adj.* 出生於
She was born in the United States.
她在美國出生。

. . . .

❸ **special** /ˋspɛʃəl/ *adj.* 特別的
What's so special about this place?
這個地方特別在哪裡？

. . . .

❹ **accident** /ˋæksədənt/ *n.* 意外
My friend got into an accident last night.
我朋友昨天發生意外。

. . . .

❺ **control** /kənˋtrol/ *v.* 控制
You need to learn to control yourself.
你需要學著控制自己。

一句一句練習說　MP3 011 ▶

What do you enjoy doing?
你喜歡做什麼？

Communication

❶ I enjoy reading.
我喜歡看書。

❷ I enjoy singing.
我喜歡唱歌。

❸ I enjoy singing.
我喜歡唱歌。

❹ I enjoy dancing.
我喜歡跳舞。

❺ I enjoy doing crafts.
我喜歡做手工藝。

 主題單字心智圖 MP3 012 ▶

enjoy /ɪn`dʒɔɪ/ *v.* 享受

I enjoy camping with my family.
我喜歡和我的家人一起露營。

dance /dæns/ *v.* 跳舞

We are going to dance at the party.
我們要在派對上跳舞。

act /ækt/ *v.* 演戲

He's really good at acting.
他很會演戲。

sing /sɪŋ/ *v.* 唱歌

She has a talent for singing.
她很有唱歌天份。

craft /kræft/ *n.* 工藝

The town is famous for arts and crafts.
那個城鎮的藝術與工藝很有名。

Unit 4 冰雪奇緣 Frozen

Friends All Around You
朋友相伴度難關

帶著寶貝一起讀

　　有時候當我們遇到困難的時候，會選擇躲起來，試著想要自己解決一切。有時候這行得通，但很多時候只靠自己的力量真的解決不了問題。當我們自己無法解決問題時，不要忘記周遭還有很多人願意給你建議和幫助，讓你能更快度過難關喔！透過朋友和家人的幫助，讓你在困境中更感到一絲溫暖。下次遇到困難的時候，記得試著開口尋求幫助喔！

Parents

Grandparents

 主題小劇場 MP3 013 ▶

When Elsa **runs off** after she accidentally **freeze**s her kingdom, Anna goes after her on a horse, alone. Anna's horse has spooked away by falling snow and Anna **gets lost** in the icy mountains. On her journey, Anna meets an ice harvester named, Kristoff and his reindeer, Sven, at a shop. Anna convinces Kristoff to take her up the mountains. On the way, a pack of wolves attacks them. They help each other and lose the wolves. They then **meet** a snowman, Olaf, who is created by Elsa. Olaf sacrifices himself to keep Anna safe on the journey. With her friends' help, Anna is able to escape death and save her sister, Elsa. Finally, Elsa learns to open her heart and control of her powers with the help of her sister and people **around** her.

　　艾莎（Elsa）在不小心冰凍了她的王國之後逃跑，安娜（Anna）獨自騎上馬出發，想追回艾莎。安娜的馬被落下的雪嚇到，而她也在白雪覆蓋的山中迷路。在旅途中，安娜在一間店遇到採冰人阿克（Kristoff）和他的馴鹿小斯（Sven）。當一群狼攻擊他們，他們幫助彼此，擺脫了狼群。他們之後又一起遇到艾莎創造的雪人雪寶（Olaf），在旅途中，雪寶願意犧牲自己，確保安娜的安全。在朋友的幫忙之下，安娜得已逃過死亡，並拯救姊姊艾莎。艾莎也在妹妹和其他人的幫忙之下，打開心房，並找到控制自己魔法的方法。

 故事單字一起學　MP3 014 ▶

1 **run off** /rʌn ɔf/ *ph.* 逃跑

I will not run off when things get hard.

當遇到困難的時候，我不會逃跑。

2 **freeze** /friz/ *v.* 結冰

Water freezes at 0℃.

水在攝氏零度時結冰。

3 **get lost** /kɛr/ *ph.* 迷路

Her two children got lost in the aquarium.

她兩個小孩在水族館裡面迷路了。

4 **meet** /mit/ *v.* 相遇、見面

We are going to meet at the station.

我們會在車站碰面。

5 **around** /əˋraʊnd/ *prep.* 在…四周

You can count on your friends around you.

你可以依靠你周遭的朋友。

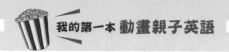
 一句一句練習說 MP3 015 ▶

What does a friend do?
一個朋友會做什麼？

Communication

❶ **A friend listens to you.**
朋友會聽你說話。

❷ **A friend cares about you.**
朋友會關心你。

❸ **A friend forgives you.**
朋友會原諒你。

❹ **A friend spends time with you.**
朋友會花時間和你在一起。

❺ **A friend is always there for you.**
朋友會一直支持你。

 **主題單字心智圖** MP3 016 ▶

listen /ˈlɪsn/ *v.* 聽

Are you listening to me？
你有在聽我說話嗎？

friend /frɛnd/ n. 朋友

He is my best friend.
他是我最好的朋友。

care /mɪt/ *v.* 關懷

Parents care about their children.
父母關心他們的孩子。

spend /spɛnd/ *v.* 花費（時間、金錢）

Jane spent 2 hours doing her homework last night.
珍昨晚花了兩小時寫作業。

forgive /fəˈgɪv/ *v.* 原諒

I think I will forgive him.
我想我會原諒他。

帶著寶貝一起讀

當我們待在家中，身邊有我們最親愛的家人和朋友陪伴我們，但是我們也許有一天會離開我們熟悉的地方，例如搬家、轉學與熟悉的朋友說再見，這都讓人很緊張又害怕。擔心自己無法適應，害怕遇到很多新的事情。但隨著我們長大了，變得更強壯後，我們可以試著勇敢跨出一步，離開習慣的環境，到新的地方旅行或是生活，遇見新的朋友，讓自己的人生更豐富唷！ 就像尼莫（Nemo）和爸爸馬林（Marlin）離開熟悉的珊瑚礁，雖然一路上遇到許多困難，但這趟冒險也讓他們父子倆更加親近，成長許多呢！

Parents

Grandparents

 主題小劇場　MP3 017 ▶

Due to a tragic event, the clownfish, Nemo is the only child left in the family that lives in the Great Barrier Reef. His father, Marlin, is therefore very protective of Nemo. On the first day of school, Marlin helps Nemo get ready and **worries** whether Nemo can **take care of** himself. Nemo is curious about the world outside of the home, so he always asks a lot of questions about the big world to Marlin. Marlin fails to give any answers every time because he doesn't **leave** their home — the Great Barrier Reef after his wife's death.

Nemo's teacher takes the class on a field trip, and Marlin follows because he is worried about where they are going. Nemo sneaks away while his father is talking to the teacher. Nemo ends up in a fish tank in a dentist's office. Marlin swims everywhere trying to find Nemo. Nemo eventually manages to **reunite** with his father. Nemo has learned a lot from the **adventure** and Marlin can provide answers to Nemo's previous questions.

　　因為一場悲劇，小丑魚尼莫（Nemo）成為家庭裡唯一的孩子，他的父親馬林（Marlin）因此非常保護他。在上學的第一天，尼莫非常興奮。馬林幫忙尼莫準備，同時也擔心尼莫有沒有辦法照顧自己。尼莫對大堡礁外面的世界很好奇，所以他總是問他爸爸許多有關外面世界的問題，但馬林都無法回答因為他自從妻子過世後就沒有離開家─大堡礁了。

　　尼莫的老師帶學生去校外教學，馬林對他們要去的地方感到不安，而跟上前。尼莫趁爸爸和老師說話的時候，偷偷溜走。結果尼莫被帶到牙醫診所裡的魚缸裡，而他的父親則到處找他。尼莫最終得以和父親相聚，尼莫在這趟冒險旅程中學了很多，而馬林也終於能回答尼莫關於這個世界的各種問題了。

 故事單字一起學　MP3 018 ▶

❶ **worry** /ˈwɝɪ/ *v.* 擔心
You have nothing to worry about.
你不用擔心任何事情。

❷ **take care of** /tek kɛr əv/ *ph.* 照顧
My son helps take care of our dog.
我的兒子會幫忙照顧我們的狗。

❸ **leave** /liːv/ *v.* 離開
I'll be leaving at five o'clock tomorrow.
我明天早晨五點鐘離開。

❹ **reunite** /rijuˈnaɪt/ *v.* 重聚
After two weeks, he finally reunited with his parents.
過了兩週，他終於能回到父母身邊。

❺ **adventure** /ədˈvɛntʃɚ/ *n.* 冒險
Let's take on an adventure!
我們一起去冒險吧！

一句一句練習說　MP3 019 ▶

When do you feel nervous?
什麼情況下你會感到緊張？

Communication

❶ I feel nervous when I sing.
我唱歌的時候會緊張。

❷ I feel nervous when I talk to new people.
和不認識的人說話我會緊張。

❸ I feel nervous when I travel to a new place.
旅行到一個新地方我會緊張。

❹ I feel nervous when I go to a new school.
到新學校我會緊張。

❺ I feel nervous when I take a test.
我考試的時候會緊張。

 主題單字心智圖 MP3 020 ▶

nervous /ˈnɝ·vəs/ adj. 緊張的
Talking in public makes me nervous.
演說讓我緊張。

new /nju/ adj. 新的
I got a new toy last week.
我上週拿到一個新玩具。

place /ples/ n. 地方
That is my favorite place.
那是我最喜歡的地方。

people /ˈpip!/ n. 人們
There are a lot of people in the restaurant.
餐廳裡人很多。

test /tɛst/ n. 考試
We have a test every morning.
我們每天早上都有考試。

Unit 6 史瑞克三世 Shrek the Third
Let Go Of Outside Expectations
擺脫外界期望

帶著寶貝一起讀

你想過長大後成為什麼樣的人嗎？爸媽和周遭的人都對我們有期望，希望我們認真讀書，每次都考第一名，成為一名醫生或是鋼琴演奏家。這些期望自有它的道理，但如果你已經努力讀書了，還是每次都考得不甚理想，不要因此太難過和自責。很多時候我們也會不自覺被期望限制，不小心就忘記我們真正想做的事和興趣，找尋屬於自己的天賦吧！多想自己擅長的事或真正的興趣吧！相信你可以和電影裡的史瑞克（Shrek）或亞瑟（Arthur）一樣，在努力地尋覓後，找到自己真正的興趣。

Parents

Grandparents

 主題小劇場　MP3 021 ▶

In the land of Far, Far Away, **King** Harold is very sick. If he passes away, his son-in-law Shrek and his daughter Fiona will become King and Queen. Shrek doesn't think that he should be King and someone else should rule the kingdom. Before King Harold's last breathe, he reveals that there is another **heir**, Fiona's cousin, Arthur. Shrek sets off to find Arthur, along with some companions.

When they find Arthur in his school, they discover that he is constantly pushed around. Shrek explains why he is there. Arthur is **excited** to be the new king and leaves with Shrek. Unfortunately, some villains capture Shrek. Arthur shows great **courage** and leadership skills in his attempt to save himself, Shrek and the others. He eventually becomes King. Shrek is able to **go after** what he wants and retire to the swamp with Fiona.

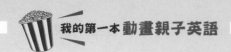

　　在「很遠很遠的王國」（Far, Far Away）裡，哈洛德國王（King Harold）病得很嚴重。在國王過世之後，女婿史瑞克（Shrek）與女兒費歐娜（Fiona）則會變成國王與王后。在國王嚥下最後一口氣之前，透露了其實還有另一個繼承人—費歐娜的表弟亞瑟（Arthur）。史瑞克和一些同伴出發尋找亞瑟。

　　當他們在亞瑟的學校找到他的時候，發現亞瑟常被欺負。史瑞克解釋了自己的出現。亞瑟很興奮可以成為新的國王，並和史瑞克一起出發。很不幸的，壞人抓住了史瑞克，亞瑟則在拯救自己、史瑞克和其他人的同時，展現了極大的勇氣與領導能力，最終他順利成為國王，而史瑞克也得以尋找自己的目標，並和費歐娜退休回沼澤。

 故事單字一起學　MP3 022 ▶

1 **king** /kɪŋ/ *n.* 國王
People wonder who will be the next king.
人們想知道誰是下一位國王。

2 **heir** /ɛr/ *n.* 繼承人
She is the heir to the kingdom.
她是這個王國的繼承人。

3 **excited** /ɪkˋsaɪtɪd/ *adj.* 興奮的
He is very excited about studying abroad.
要出國唸書了，他很興奮。

4 **courage** /ˏkɝɪdʒ/ *n.* 勇氣
It takes courage to be who you really are.
當自己是需要勇氣的。

5 **go after** /go ˋæftɚ/ *ph.* 追求
She decided to go after her dreams.
她決定去追求自己的夢想。

What do you want to be when you grow up?
你長大想做什麼？

Communication

❶ I want to be a singer.
我要當歌手。

❷ I want to be a teacher.
我要當老師。

❸ I want to be a doctor.
我要當醫生。

❹ I want to be a basketball player.
我要當籃球選手。

❺ I want to be a fire fighter.
我要當消防員。

 主題單字心智圖　MP3 024 ▶

basketball /ˈbæskɪtˌbɔl/ *n.* 籃球
We always play basketball together.
我們總是一起打籃球。

grow up *ph.* 長大
I can't wait to grow up.
我等不及要長大了。

teacher /ˈtitʃɚ/ *n.* 老師
She is our new teacher.
她是我們的新老師。

firefighter /ˈfaɪrˌfaɪtɚ/ *n.* 消防員
A firefighter puts out fires.
消防員負責滅火。

doctor /ˈdɑktɚ/ *n.* 醫生
You need to see a doctor.
你需要去看醫生。

帶著寶貝一起讀

　　電影裡的超能先生（Mr. Incredible）一直懷念著過去的光榮，完全沒有將心思放在家人身上。雖然過去和未來都很重要，你要記的更重要的是「當下」，假設我們在散步的時候，擔心作業還沒完成，寫作業的時候卻在想昨天玩的遊戲，不專心的結果是很多事都沒有好好完成。多把注意力放在現在，珍惜當下，例如：和家人朋友聊天的時候，認真的對話，在吃東西的時候，專心地品嘗食物，一定會有很多出乎意料之外的新發現喔！你今天發現了什麼呢？

Parents

Grandparents

 MP3 025 ▶

Mr. Incredible was one of the most respected superheroes. He spent all his time saving people and animals. Sometimes he would help the police catch bank robbers and on the way, he would save an old lady's cat. That was how amazing he was until an accident **force**d him to retire and live as the normal white-collar worker, Bob Parr. He cannot do anything that will tell people he is a superhero. He has to live like a normal person and act like everyone else. He has difficulties **forget**ting the glorious past and dislikes his ordinary life and job. Everything in his life now makes him angry. The only thing that interests him is the newspaper because he can read about crimes. One night at dinner, Bob is reading the newspaper again. After his son is sent to the principal's office, his wife wants Bob to talk to their son and tell their son to behave well. Before the **conversation** between Bob and his wife can go anywhere, Bob goes to his secret plan with his former superhero friends. They listen to police radio and Bob waits for the chance to be a superhero again. Later when Bob secretly uses his superpower to take a part-time job, he accidentally puts himself in danger and his family comes to save him with no doubt. This is the moment he realizes and he **regret**s obsessing over his past and not **paying attention** to his family who is always beside him.

　　「超能先生」（Mr. Incredible）是最受尊重的超級英雄之一，他所有的時間都在拯救人們與動物。有時候他會幫忙警方捕捉銀行搶匪，並在半路上先解救老婆婆的小貓，他就是那麼的厲害，直到他被迫退休，以平凡的上班族「巴鮑伯」（Bob Parr）的身份過著生活。現在的他不能做任何會讓人知道他是超級英雄的事，他必須和其他人一樣生活。他無法忘掉光榮的過去，對現在平凡的生活和工作感到厭倦。現在生活裡的一切都讓他生氣，唯一讓他感興趣的東西只有報紙，因為他能看看發生了什麼案件。有一天吃晚餐時，鮑伯又在看報紙了。在兒子被叫進校長室之後，他的太太希望鮑伯能和兒子談談，叫他乖一點，但是在鮑伯和太太的對話能有個頭緒之前，鮑伯就和以前的超級英雄朋友一起秘密聚會，他們都在偷聽警方的無線電，而鮑伯則等著可以再成為超級英雄的機會。當鮑伯偷偷再次使用超能力打工時，卻意外導致自己陷入危險，他的家人二話不說趕來拯救他，這時他才開始後悔自己一直陷在過去，沒有好好關心一直陪伴在身邊的家人。

 故事單字一起學　MP3 026 ▶

❶ **force** /fors/ *v.* 強迫
You can't force me to leave.
你不能強迫我離開。

❷ **forget** /fəˋgɛt/ *v.* 忘記
Don't forget to lock the door.
不要忘記鎖門。

❸ **conversation** /ˌkɑnvəˋseʃən/ *n.* 會話
I overheard her conversation with Ryan.
我不小心聽到她和瑞恩的對話。

❹ **regret** /rɪˋgrɛt/ *v.* 後悔
I regret not going to Japan with them.
我很後悔沒跟他們去日本。

❺ **pay attention** /pent əˈten.ʃən/ *ph.* 注意
I plan to pay more attention to my health.
我計畫多注意我的健康。

一句一句練習說　MP3 027 ▶

What are you doing now?
你現在正在做什麼？

Communication

❶ I am talking to my friend.
我在和我朋友聊天。

❷ I am having dinner with my family.
我在和我家人吃飯。

❸ I am reading a book.
我在看書。

❹ I'm watching a movie.
我在看電影。

❺ I'm painting.
我在畫畫。

 主題單字心智圖　MP3 028 ▶

dinner /ˈdɪnɚ/ *n.* 晚餐

He cooks dinner for her every evening.
他每天傍晚幫她煮晚餐。

talk /tɔk/ *v.* 講話

Let's talk about the book.
我們來談談這本書。

read /ri:d/ *v.* 閱讀

Reading helps me relax.
閱讀讓我放鬆。

movie /ˈmuvɪ/ *n.* 電影

The Incredibles is my favorite movie.
《超人特攻隊》是我最喜歡的電影。

paint /pent/ *v.* 繪畫

She painted a portrait of herself.
她畫了一幅自畫像。

Your Greatest Support System
家人是你最堅強的支柱

帶著寶貝一起讀

　　人生中，會遇到許多困難，或突然心情不好，可是千萬不要以為自己孤單一個人，轉過頭，你的家人都在默默地支持你、愛著你，有了家人的支持，很多難關會更容易度過的。辛苦的時候，想想你的家人吧！你有仔細觀察過你家人的長相或行為嗎？上次你對家人說「我愛你」是什麼時候呢？親近的家人，可能因為長時間相處，容易吵架，但彼此一直陪伴在身邊，因為這份深厚的感情，就從現在開始，多多擁抱你的家人，表達你對他們最深的感謝和愛吧！

Parents

Grandparents

Bob Parr is previously known as Mr. Incredible. During his forced retirement, he can't stand his normal and boring life. He seeks chances to **save** people from **danger** as a superhero.

One day, a mysterious woman contacts Bob. She gives him an opportunity to take on a mission to kill a dangerous robot on a remote island. He will be given more money and more missions like this if he becomes the superhero again.

However, all of this is a trap. A villain is looking to kill Mr. Incredible and other super-heroes. His **wife**, who is also a superhero, finds out and sets out to save him. Their two older **kid**s, who also have super-powers, secretly follow. On the island, the whole super-hero family **supports** and rescues each other in the face of danger.

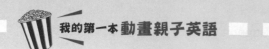

　　巴鮑伯（Bob Parr）是以前的超能先生（Mr. Incredible），在他被迫退休後，他無法忍受自己平凡無聊的生活，一直想找機會再以超級英雄的身份拯救人類。有一天，一個神秘女子連絡上他，她提供一個接下一項任務的機會，到一個遙遠的小島殺死一隻危險的機器人。他後續可以得到更多錢與任務就像他再次成為超級英雄一樣。

　　但沒想到這一切都是個陷阱，有個壞人想殺掉超能先生和其他超級英雄。他同樣是超級英雄的太太聽到了消息，前去拯救他，而他們也擁有超能力的兩個年紀較大的小孩也偷偷跟去。在島上，當面對危險時，這超級英雄一家人互相支持並拯救彼此。

 故事單字一起學　MP3 030 ▶

❶ save /sev/ *v.* 拯救
You saved the day.
你讓我們度過難關。

- -

❷ danger /ˋdendʒɚ/ *n.* 危險
He didn't know his life was in danger.
他不知道他的生命受到了威脅。

- -

❸ wife /waɪf/ *n.* 太太
I finally get to meet his wife.
我終於可以見到他太太。

- -

❹ kid /kɪd/ *n.* 小孩
The father always takes his kids to the park.
那位父親總是帶他小孩去公園。

- -

❺ support /səˋport/ *v.* 支持
We all support your decision.
我們都支持你的決定。

一句一句練習說　MP3 031 ▶

What does your sister look like?
你姊姊（妹妹）長什麼樣子？

Communication

❶ My sister is tall.
我的姊姊很高。

❷ She is a slim girl.
她很纖瘦。

❸ My sister has long straight hair.
我的姊姊有一頭很長的直髮。

❹ She has very big eyes.
她的眼睛很大。

❺ She has a beautiful smile.
她笑起來很美。

 主題單字心智圖 MP3 032 ▶

slim /slɪm/ *adj.* 纖細的

My neighbor is a slim boy with long hair.
我的鄰居是個有頭長髮的瘦瘦的男生。

tall /tɔl/ *adj.* 高的

He is growing taller.
他越長越高。

straight /stret/ *adj.* 直的

Please draw a straight line.
請畫一條直線。

smile /smaɪl/ *n.* 笑容

Don't forget to smile.
別忘了要微笑。

hair /hɛr/ *n.* 頭髮

I wash my hair every day.
我每天洗頭髮。

Unity Is Strength
團結力量大

帶著寶貝一起讀

　　我們都必須學習獨自完成一個任務，像自己整理書包、自己完成作業等。但不一定所有事情和問題我們都能自己解決，我們需要跟他人合作。從小學習團隊合作和「團隊精神」，因為與人合作不是一件簡單的事，透過合作能想到許多一個人想不出的好主意，幫助更快解決問題。團結力量大，一起行動，我們能做出更大的改變。想想最近有沒有遇到什麼問題，可不可以找人一起解決呢？

Parents　　**Grandparents**

 主題小劇場 MP3 033 ▶

Due to a dispute between Mike and Sulley, they are expelled from the scaring program in their university. To go back into the program, they and their other team **member**s join the scare game. In the first round of the game, Mike and Sulley are so focused on making themselves win that they lose as a **team**. Luckily, one team gets disqualified and Mike and Sulley's team can advance to the next round.

In the following round, Sulley causes troubles because he doesn't **trust** his team members. The rest of the team work together and help the team advance again. Even though there are countless **challenge**s, Mike and Sulley both come to the realization that by working **together**, they can make a great team and reach their goals.

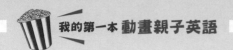

　　大眼仔（Mike）和毛怪（Sulley）因為兩人之間的爭執被趕出了驚嚇系。為了回到驚嚇系，兩人和他們其他的隊員一起參加驚嚇遊戲。在遊戲的第一輪，大眼仔和毛怪因為太想為自己贏得勝利，反而導致整隊輸掉比賽。所幸有一隊被取消資格，大眼仔和毛怪的隊伍得以晉級。

　　在比賽第二輪，毛怪因為不相信隊員而闖禍，但整隊互相幫忙，又得以再次晉級。雖然在這之後還遇到很多挑戰，但大眼仔和毛怪都發現原來只要兩人一起合作，便可以成為優秀的團隊，達成目標。

 故事單字一起學　MP3 034 ▶

❶ member /ˋmɛmbɚ/ *n.* 成員
Some members of the group don't trust the leader.
有些團隊成員不相信領導者。

❷ team /tim/ *n.* 隊伍
We should work as a team.
我們應該要團隊合作。

❸ trust /trʌst/ *v.* 信任
You need to trust yourself.
你要相信自己。

❹ challenge /ˋtʃælɪndʒ/ *n.* 挑戰
I will help you overcome the challenge.
我會幫你克服困難。

❺ together /təˈgeðə(r)/ *adv.* 共同
We go camping together every weekend.
我們每個週末都一起去露營。

一句一句練習說 MP3 035 ▶

Communication

Why should people work together?
為什麼人們要合作？

❶ We can help each other.
我們可以幫助彼此。

❷ We can learn from each other.
我們可以互相學習。

❸ We can learn to talk to each other.
學會和彼此溝通。

❹ We can be stronger.
我們可以變得更強大。

❺ We can solve bigger problems.
我們可以解決更大的問題。

 主題單字心智圖　MP3 036 ▶

learn /lɝn/ *v.* 學習

I can learn a lot from books.
我可以從書上學到很多。

each other /ˌitʃ ˋʌðɚ/ *ph.* 彼此

My friend and I see each other every week.
我朋友和我每週見面。

strong /strɔŋ/ *adj.* 強壯的

He is a strong person.
他很強壯。

animal /ˋænəm!/ *n.* 動物

We should take care of the animals.
我們應該照顧小動物。

talkative /ˋtɔkətɪv/ *adj.* 健談的

I want to learn to be more talkative.
我想學著多說一點話。

Unit 10 怪獸大學 Monsters University
Stick To Your Dreams
堅持夢想不放棄

🎞 帶著寶貝一起讀

　　夢想是個很美麗的東西，但達成夢想的道路就不一定美麗，完成夢想要花很多時間努力。有的人很快可以達成夢想，有的人需要花上很多的時間，就像想成為「驚嚇員」的大眼仔（Mike），花了好久才找到方法完成夢想。不管怎樣，他還是都不斷的堅持，將前往夢想的道路，切割成一個一個的目標，慢慢往前，想著家人與朋友，相信有一天會完成美麗的夢想。記住，前往夢想的道路不只一條喔！你的夢想是什麼呢？想想可以怎麼達到吧！

Parents

Grandparents

 MP3 037 ▶

When Mike the monster is young, he visits Monsters Inc. on a school field trip. He is inspired to become a scarer that harvests children's screams to generate power.When Mike grows up, he starts school at Monsters University. Everyone in the university **makes fun of** him. Although people think that he will **never** become a scarer because he is not scary at all, he studies hard and practices. Unfortunately, he is kicked out of the scaring program because he is not scary enough. He follows the rules too hard and forgets to see his own advantages.

He is not defeated. He finds a way to join the scare game to **prove** that he can be scary. Moreover, he finds that winning the scare game can help him go back to the scaring program. Despite the ups and downs, Mike **sticks to** his **dream**. Even though things don't go as planned, he manages to starts work at Monsters Inc. and, by teaming up with Sulley, works his way up to the scare floor.

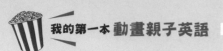

怪獸大眼仔（Mike）小的時候，因為學校戶外教學，他得以參觀怪獸電力公司，在這趟旅程他受到激發，決心成為一名專門收集小孩尖叫聲來發電的「驚嚇員」。

大眼仔長大之後進了怪獸大學唸書。在大學裡，每個人都取笑他。雖然大家說他不可能成為驚嚇員，但他還是很認真唸書和練習。不幸的是，他卻因為不夠恐怖而被踢出驚嚇系。他太拘泥規矩了，而忘記看看自己的優點。

大眼仔沒有被打敗，他找到方法參加驚嚇遊戲來證明自己是恐怖的，除此之外，他發現贏得驚嚇遊戲可以幫助他回到驚嚇系。雖然歷經曲折，他還是堅持自己的夢想。即使事情不如他原本計劃的進行，他想辦法進到怪獸電力公司工作，並和毛怪合作無堅，進到夢想的驚嚇樓層。

 故事單字一起學　MP3 038 ▶

1 **make fun of** /mek fʌn əf/ *ph.* 取笑
It's not nice to make fun of people.
取笑別人是不好的。

2 **never** /ˋnɛvɚ/ *adv.* 從不
I have never been to Europe.
我從沒去過歐洲。

3 **prove** /pruv/ *v.* 證明
He works hard to prove himself.
他很努力證明自己。

4 **stick to** /stɪkˈtu/ *ph.* 堅持
It's important that we stick to our plan.
固守我們的計劃是很重要的。

5 **dream** /drim/ *n.* 夢、夢想
I had a very strange dream last night.
我昨天做了一個奇怪的夢。

How do you reach your goals?
你如何可以達到目標？

Communication

❶ I will talk about my goals.
我會告訴別人我的目標。

❷ I will trust myself.
我要相信我自己。

❸ I will keep learning.
我會一直不斷學習。

❹ I will wait.
我會等待。

❺ I'll find a reward.
我會幫自己想一個獎賞。

 主題單字心智圖　MP3 040 ▶

reach /ritʃ/ *v.* 伸手碰到

I can't reach the book.
我拿不到那本書。

keep /kip/ *v.* 持續不斷

Just keep going and you will be there.
不斷往前，你就可以成功。

goal /gol/ *n.* 目標

My goal is to jog every day.
我的目標是每天慢跑。

wait /weit/ *v.* 等

Can you wait a second?
可以等一下下嗎？

reward /rɪˋwɔrd/ *n.* 獎賞

There's a reward for finishing the work.
完成工作後會有獎賞。

Put Yourself in Their Shoes
從他們角度想一想

帶著寶貝一起讀

　　你有沒有看過有人因為害怕或好玩，傷害了一些昆蟲或動物呢？你有沒有什麼感覺？有時候我們因為不得已，必須趕走這些昆蟲或動物，我們怕會生病或是我們怕會被咬，不過我們要記住，這片土地不是只屬於人類的，當我們有大片的土地可以生活或玩耍，我們應該要更常抱著尊重跟謙遜的心，對待其他的動物與植物。抱著尊重的心，設身處地，多多為跟我一起生活在地球上的動物或植物著想，永續保護我們的地球。

Parents

Grandparents

 主題小劇場 MP3 041 ▶

There are three brothers, Sitka, Denahi and Kenai. One day, Kenai is responsible for tying a basket of fish on the tree but the basket falls off. When he and his brothers return, the fish are taken away. Kenai thinks it is a **bear** and he goes out to find the bear. His brothers follow. Kenai throws rocks at the bear and this anger the bear. Kenai's two brothers try to save him. Sitka falls off the cliff to save his brothers. Even though Denahi says it is not the bear's fault, Kenai is very angry at the bear and leaves to kill it. Right after he kills the bear, Kenai is turned **into** a bear.

Kenai wakes up as a bear and is very surprised. To change back to a human being, he needs to find his brother, Sitka, on the top of the **mountain**. He steps into a hunter's trap and meets a little bear **cub** named Koda, who cannot find his mother. Koda promises to take Kenai to where he needs to be. Suddenly, Denahi runs toward Kenai, who is now a bear. Denahi comes to kill the bear that kills Kenai, but he does not know that the bear is actually Kenai. Kenai runs away from Denahi. He sets on a journey with Koda to the top of the mountain. Kenai and Koda save each other from Denahi. Kenai is very surprised when Koda says that people are scary monsters because Kenai always thinks bears are monsters. When they reach the top of the mountain, Denahi finds them. Kenai tries to protect Koda from Denahi and turns back into a human being. Kenai finally understands that animals can love, too. He learns to love all **living** things. In the end, he decides to stay as a bear and be with Koda.

　　有三兄弟小奇（Sitka）、狄克（Denahi）和肯尼（Kenai）。有一天肯尼負責把一籃魚綁在樹上，但籃子掉了下來，當肯尼和哥哥回來的時候，魚已經被拿走了。肯尼覺得是熊偷的，跑去找熊，他的哥哥趕緊跟上。肯尼對著熊丟石頭，惱怒了熊，他的兩個哥哥試著要救他，小奇為了救弟弟，最後掉下懸崖。雖然狄克說這不是熊的錯，但肯尼還是非常的生氣，並跑去把熊殺了。肯尼一把熊殺了，他就變成了一隻熊。肯尼醒來之後變成一隻熊非常驚訝，如果想要變回人，他必須在山頂找到自己的哥哥小奇。他踩進了獵人的陷阱，並遇到了一隻叫哥達（Koda）的小熊，小熊和媽媽走失了。哥達答應要帶肯尼去他要去的地方。突然狄克衝向已經變成熊的肯尼，狄克是來為肯尼報仇，但他卻不知道這隻熊其實是肯尼。肯尼趕快逃離狄克。他和哥達出發前往山頂，途中肯尼和哥達幫助對方，不受到狄克的傷害，肯尼聽到哥達說人是怪物的時候，他很驚訝，因為一直以來肯尼都覺得熊才是怪獸。當他們抵達山頂的時候，狄克找到了他們，肯尼試著要保護哥達，突然變回了人類。肯尼終於了解動物們也懂得愛，也學會要愛護所有生物，最後他決定當一隻熊，留在柯達身邊。

故事單字一起學 MP3 042 ▶

❶ **bear** /bɛr/ *n.* 熊
The hunter saw a bear.
那個獵人看到了一隻熊。

. . . .

❷ **turn into** /tɜ˞n `ɪntu/ *ph.* 變成
The tadpole turned into a frog.
那隻蝌蚪變成一隻青蛙。

. . . .

❸ **mountain** /`maʊntn/ *n.* 山
He is going to climb the highest mountain.
她要去爬最高的山。

. . . .

❹ **cub** /kʌb/ *n.* （熊、師、虎等）幼獸
The panda just gave birth to a cub.
那隻貓熊剛剛生了一隻寶寶。

. . . .

❺ **living** /`lɪvɪŋ/ *adj.* 活著的
All living things depend on each other.
所有的生物都互相依賴彼此。

一句一句練習說　MP3 043 ▶

Communication

How do you protect living things?
你可以怎麼保護生物呢？

❶ You can plant more trees.
你可以多種一點樹。

❷ I will pick up my garbage.
我會把我的垃圾撿起來。

❸ I never take long showers.
我洗澡從不洗太久。

❹ I always bring reusable bags.
我都有帶環保袋。

❺ Don't get too close to wild animals.
不要太靠近野生動物。

 主題單字心智圖　MP3 044 ▶

tree /tri/ *n.* 樹木

They will cut down all the trees.
他們會把樹全部砍掉。

shower /ˈʃaʊɚ/ *n.* 淋浴

She is taking a shower.
她正在洗澡。

garbage /ˈɡɑrbɪdʒ/ *n.* 垃圾

Please take out the garbage.
請幫忙丟垃圾。

reusable /rɪˈjuzəbl̩/ *adj.* 能重複使用的

I bought some reusable straws for us.
我幫我們買了一些環保吸管。

close /klos/ *adj.* 近的

I live very close to my school.
我家離學校很近。

Unit 12　食破天驚 Cloudy with a Chance of Meatballs
Nature Strikes Back
大自然的反撲

帶著寶貝一起讀

　　從以前到現在，我們的生活裡出現了許多讓我們生活變得更方便或有趣的發明，例如車子、冰箱、遊戲機等，很難想像沒有了這些東西，我們的生活會變得如何。你或許以為只有很聰明和厲害的人才能當發明家，其實所有的人，包括小朋友，都可以當發明家，就像電影裡面的弗林，發現問題，然後勇敢地嘗試，並且相信自己，大家都能成為發明家。就從現在開始，好好觀察，和家人一起想想周遭哪些地方可以變得更好、更方便，並討論可以怎麼做，可能你就是下一個偉大的發明家喔！

Parents

Grandparents

In a town called Swallow Falls lives a little boy named Flint. Flint is very interested in **invent**ing new things. He can always see the problems which people are facing. He has passion for his dream and a warm heart to help people. When he is at a very young age, and he starts to **create** something that can help people **solve** the problems. One day, he notices children's untied shoelaces and invents spray-on shoes. With spray-on shoes, people will not have to worry about shoelaces anymore. Although spray-on shoes fail because you cannot take them off, Flint does not **give up** on his passion for inventing things.

He always believes that he can invent something to say thanks to his mother. His mother helps him to have great confidence. After this, he spends a lot of time in his own **lab** and inventing even more things. Sadly, none of the things work well and people think that he is only causing troubles, but this does not stop Flint. When he sees how the people in his town are left with only one kind of food to eat, he knows what he can do to help. He will create a machine that is going to bring people all kinds of food.

在一個叫燕瀑島（Swallow Falls）的小鎮上，住著一個名叫佛林（Flint）的小男孩。他對發明新東西非常有興趣。即使年紀很小，他總是可以看出人們遇到的問題，然後試著創造出可以幫助人們解決問題的東西。有一天，他注意到小孩沒綁的鞋帶，並發明了「立噴鞋」，有了「立噴鞋」，人們再也不用擔心鞋帶了。雖然因為穿上就脫不下來，「立噴鞋」失敗了，但是佛林完全沒有失去對發明的熱愛。

因為他的母親，他一直都相信自己有一天可以做出一個偉大的發明，他的母親幫助她學會相信自己。後來他花了很多時間在自己的實驗室裡，創造出更多的東西。很可惜的是，沒有一樣東西成功，而且人們都覺得他只會製造麻煩，但這並沒有阻止佛林。當他看到鎮裡的人只能吃一種食物的時候，他知道他可以怎麼幫忙，他要製造一台可以給人們帶來各種食物的機器。

 故事單字一起學　MP3 046 ▶

❶ **invent** /ɪn`vɛnt/ *v.* 發明
Thomas Edison invented the light bulb.
湯瑪斯・愛迪生發明了燈泡。

❷ **create** /krɪ`et/ *v.* 創造
They create a lot of useful tools.
他們創造出很多有用的工具。

❸ **solve** /sɔlv/ *v.* 解決
I don't know how to solve this problem.
我不知道該如何解決這個問題。

❹ **give up** /gɪv ʌp/ *ph.* 放棄
Keep trying! Don't give up.
繼續嘗試！不要放棄。

❺ **lab** /læb/ *n.* 實驗室
She invented that machine in this lab.
她是在這個實驗室發明那台機器的。

一句一句練習說　MP3 047 ▶

@#$%^

What can you do with your computer?
你可以用電腦做什麼？

Communication

❶ I can use it to do my homework.
我可以用電腦寫作業。

❷ I can use it to find information.
我可以用電腦來找資料。

❸ I can use it to view photos.
我可以用電腦來看照片。

❹ I can use it to listen to music.
我可以用電腦來聽音樂。

❺ I can use it to learn.
我可以用電腦來學習。

 主題單字心智圖　MP3 048 ▶

computer /kəmˋpjutɚ/ *n.* 電腦

I always do my homework on my computer.
我常常用電腦寫作業。

homework /ˋhomˌwɝk/ *n.* 作業

Please turn in your homework.
請繳交你的作業。

information /ˌɪnfɚˋmeʃən/ *n.* 資訊

She will give us some useful information.
她會提供我們一些有用的資訊。

photo /ˋfoto/ *n.* 照片

Let me take a photo of you first.
我先幫你們拍張照。

view /vju/ *v.* 觀看

Millions of people viewed the video.
許多人看了那部影片。

帶著寶貝一起讀

　　你有觀察過你每天丟掉的食物嗎？

　　其實不管是家庭、學校或商店，每天都有許多被丟掉的食物。當我們生活的地方食物過剩時，地球的另一頭，卻有人過著毫無食物可以吃的日子。我們的食物如此地分配不均，造成食物充沛的地區，不懂珍惜，隨便就丟掉吃不完或放到過期的食物;而沒有食物吃的地區，就只能每天處於飢餓。身在食物充沛國家的我們，要抱著感恩的心，想辦法減少食物的浪費。想想看可以怎麼做吧！

Parents

Grandparents

 主題小劇場　MP3 049 ▶

Flint invents the machine that people put water into to create **food** that rains from the sky. It excites the people who only have sardines as their primary food. People in the town keep **asking for** all kinds of food and Flint keeps working the machine to fulfill the people's orders. Tons of food falls from the sky every day, from hamburgers to spaghetti, to pancakes and ice cream. It leads to a lot of **leftover**s. Sadly, this does not stop people from asking for more food.

In order to deal with leftovers, Flint invents another machine that sweeps up all the leftover food and shoots it into a dam. This continues for a while until the machine gets out of hand and creates a food storm. The dam cannot **hold** any more food. Food **burst**s out of the dam and washes everything away.

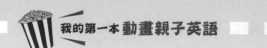

　　佛林（Flint）發明了一種機器，可以將水轉換成食物，再從空中落下。主要食物只有沙丁魚的人們十分地興奮。城鎮的人們不斷要求不同的食物，而佛林則一直讓機器運轉，滿足人們的要求。每天都有大量的食物從空中落下，從漢堡、義大利麵到鬆餅、冰淇淋。造成許多剩餘的食物，很可惜地，這並沒有阻止市民索求更多食物。

　　為了處理剩餘的食物，佛林發明另一個機器，將剩餘的食物掃起，丟進一個大壩。事情就這樣持續了一段時間，直到機器不受控制，創造出一場食物風暴，而大壩再也支撐不住，食物從大壩一瀉而出，沖垮所有事物。

 故事單字一起學　MP3 050 ▶

❶ food /fud/ *n.* 食物
I eat healthy food for every meal.
我每餐都吃健康的食物。

❷ ask for /æsk fɔr/ *ph.* 要求
She is hungry and asks for some snacks.
她肚子餓，要了一些零食。

❸ leftover /ˋleft͵ovɚ/ *n.* 廚餘
We have leftovers night every week .
我們每個星期都有剩菜之夜。

❹ hold /hold/ *v.* 容納
The bag can hold all the books.
這個包包可以裝進全部的書。

❺ burst /bɝst/ *v.* 破裂、衝出
The balloon suddenly burst.
氣球突然破掉。

一句一句練習說　MP3 051 ▶

Communication

What is your favorite food?
你最喜歡的食物是什麼？

❶ My favorite food is rice.
我最喜歡飯。

❷ My favorite food is pasta.
我最喜歡義大利麵。

❸ I like meat.
我喜歡吃肉。

❹ I love all kinds of vegetables.
各種蔬菜我都愛。

❺ I am crazy about jello.
我超愛果凍。

 主題單字心智圖　MP3 052 ▶

pasta /ˋpɑstə/ *n.* 義大利麵

There are many kinds of pasta.
義大利麵有很多種。

rice /raɪs/ *n.* 米飯

I eat a bowl of rice with every meal.
我每餐都吃一碗飯。

meat /mit/ *n.* 肉

He can't live without meat
他不能沒有肉。

vegetables /ˋvɛdʒətəb!s/ *n.* 蔬菜

Having vegetables is good for you.
吃蔬菜對你好。

jello /ˋdʒɛlo/ *n.* 果凍

She served jello after dinner.
她晚餐過後端上了果凍。

Unit 14 腦筋急轉彎 Inside Out
It's OK To Be Sad
傷心沒關係

🍋 帶著寶貝一起讀

　　面對負面情緒，想哭或生氣，我們常常被教導應該隱藏，不要哭、不要生氣。但是這樣的習慣，讓我們變成壓抑，想哭或生氣的時候只會一直忍住，跟家人或朋友也只分享開心的事。不過，這並不健康，不管正面的情緒（開心、感激）或負面情緒（生氣、挫折），都是你的情緒，都應該被正視，我們需要慢慢練習，找出適當的抒發或處理方式，以免壓抑過久，一直忍耐之後，用了錯誤的方式表達情緒。想想你每天感覺到的是哪一種情緒？想想看可以怎麼解決吧！

Parents

Grandparents

 MP3 053 ▶

Riley is **guided** by her **emotion**s, Joy, Sadness, Anger, Fear, and Disgust, that works from the Headquarters. She has to move with her family to San Fransisco. When they arrive, she is constantly disappointed by what she sees and experiences. Inside her **mind**, Joy wants to keep things **positive** about the change. She guides Riley to think about happy things and distracts her from being negative. Meanwhile, Sadness touches memories even though Joy stops her from doing anything. Unfortunately, Sadness touches a core memory, and in the struggle between Joy and Sadness, all core memories are lost. The two set out to find the core memories. During the journey, Joy realizes that Sadness is important as well. Being sad is how Riley gets support and is a normal way to express feelings to friends and family. Now each of Riley's memories is a **mix** of emotions with both happiness and sadness.

　　萊莉（Riley）由在「總部」工作的情緒們所主導：快樂（Joy，樂樂）、憂傷（Sadness，憂憂）、憤怒（Anger，怒怒）、恐懼（Fear，驚驚）以及厭惡（Disgust，厭厭）。萊莉和家人搬到了舊金山，抵達之後，萊莉不斷地被所見的和所經驗的感到失望。在她腦中，樂樂想要讓萊莉對這個改變保持樂觀，不斷引導她想開心的事，避免負面念頭。但同時，憂憂則不斷碰觸記憶，即使樂樂要她不要動。不幸地，憂憂碰觸了核心記憶，在樂樂和憂憂爭執時，所有核心記憶都被吸走。兩人出發去找回記憶，在旅途中，樂樂了解到憂憂也是很重要的，畢竟憂傷是萊莉得到親友支持的方法之一。這之後，萊莉的每個記憶都混雜著兩種情緒─快樂和傷心。

 主題單字心智圖　MP3 054 ▶

❶ guide /gaɪd/ *v.* 引導
He will guide the way for you.
他會幫你引導方向。

❷ emotion /ɪ`moʃən/ *n.* 情緒
There is no need to hold back your emotions.
你不需要壓抑你的情緒。

❸ mind /maɪnd/ *n.* 頭腦
I can't get the song out of my mind.
我的腦中一直在唱那首歌。

❹ positive /`pɑzətɪv/ *adj.* 正面的
My father is very positive about life.
我的父親對人生有很正面的態度。

❺ mix /mɪks/ *n.* 混合物
I found a mix of cookies and candy on the table.
我在桌上找到混在一起的餅乾和糖果。

一句一句練習說　MP3 055 ▶

Communication

How's your day? 你今天過得如何呢？

❶ I am happy.
　我很開心。

❷ I am sad.
　我很傷心。

❸ I feel angry.
　我很生氣。

❹ I feel scared.
　我很害怕。

❺ I feel bored.
　我覺得很無聊。

 主題單字心智圖　MP3 056 ▶

sad /sæd/ *adj.* 傷心的

She looked really sad.
她看起來很傷心。

happy /ˈhæpɪ/ *adj.* 開心的

He is happy to help.
他很樂意幫忙。

angry /ˈæŋgrɪ/ *adj.* 生氣的

She got really angry with me.
她很氣我。

bored /bord// *adj.* 無聊的

He is bored with the game.
他對這個遊戲感到無聊了。

scared /skɛrd/ *adj.* 害怕的

He is scared of the dark.
他很怕黑。

Unit 15 腦筋急轉彎 Inside Out
Communication Is the Key
溝通是關鍵

帶著寶貝一起讀

　　你常說出心裡的感受嗎？你都怎麼表達或是不說呢？溝通在關係的建立和維持是很重要的，跟家人或朋友一直相親相愛的秘訣就是誠實的把心裡的感覺或想法用正確的方式講出來。很多事情如果沒有說出來的話，別人是沒辦法了解的。像電影裡面的萊莉（Riley），離開朋友來到陌生的地方，情緒非常低落，但她沒有將這個困難告訴她的父母，導致他們之間的一些衝突。父母也要創造讓孩子感到安全、可以訴說不安的環境。 記住，溝通不是只有說，專心聆聽也很重要喔！

Parents

Grandparents

 主題小劇場　MP3 057 ▶

When Riley's father moves the whole family from Minnesota to San Fransisco, it takes a toll on Riley. At first, she tries to suppress the **feeling**s and keeps herself happy, or at least that's what Joy in her mind tells her to do. Joy stops Sadness, another of Riley's emotions, from taking control. Thus Riley's parents think that Riley is adjusting well. Shortly after, an accident happens and all that is left in her head are Anger, Disgust and Fear.

At dinner, Riley's mother tries to make conversation. Riley **shuts down** because her mind is not working as it usually does. Soon there is conflict between Riley and her parents. Failing to **communicate**, that night Riley decides to **run away**. Luckily, Joy and Sadness return, and Sadness takes over. Riley finally can expresses her sadness and her head works well again, so Riley decides to head home. She unleashes her emotions and tells her parents about the **difficulties** she's having. They decided to work it out together as a family.

　　當萊莉（Riley）的父親因為生意將全家從密尼蘇達州搬到舊金山時，對萊莉造成很大的負面影響。一開始，她試著壓抑情緒並保持開心，至少可以說她腦中的樂樂（Joy）叫她這麼做的，樂樂阻止萊莉的另一個情緒—憂憂（Sadness）控制萊莉，所以萊莉的父母以為她適應良好。

　　不久之後，意外發生，而萊莉腦中僅剩怒怒（Anger）、厭厭（Disgust）和驚驚（Fear）。晚餐時間，媽媽試著和萊莉聊天，但萊莉因為腦中運作不如往常，而拒絕溝通。很快的，萊莉和父母起了衝突。沒能交談，萊莉當天晚上決定離家出走。好險樂樂和憂憂即時返回，這時憂憂接手控制一切，萊莉終於釋放她的悲傷，大腦總部的一切運作恢復正常，所以萊莉決定回家。她釋放所有情緒，並告訴父母她所面對的困難。他們決定一家人一起面對和解決這個問題。

 故事單字一起學　MP3 058 ▶

①　feeling /ˋfilɪŋ/ *n.* 感覺
I felt a strong feeling of sadness.
我感受到一陣很強烈的憂傷。

- -

②　shut down /ˈʃʌt.daʊn/ *ph.* 關閉
They decided to shut down the factory.
他們決定關閉工廠。

- -

③　communicate /kəˋmjunəˏket/ *v.* 溝通
We use languages to communicate.
我們用語言來溝通。

- -

④　run away /rʌn əˋwe/ *ph.* 逃跑
Ben ran away from home last week.
班上週離家出走。

- -

⑤　difficulty /ˋdɪfəˏkʌltɪ/ *n.* 困難
We have no difficulty in working alone.
我單獨工作完全沒問題。

一句一句練習說 MP3 059 ▶

@#$%^

How do you feel when you are going to move to a new city?
當你要搬去一個新的城市時，你覺得如何？

Communication

❶ I feel nervous because I am going to join a new school.
因為我去新學校，我覺得很緊張。

❷ I feel excited because I will meet new people.
我覺得很興奮，因為我會遇見新的人。

❸ I feel lonely because I will miss my school friends.
我覺得很寂寞，因為我會想念我學校的朋友。

❹ I feel excited because I will have my own room.
我會很開心，因為我會有自己的房間。

❺ I am looking forward to it because I am going to explore the new city.
我很期待搬家，因為我可以探索新城市。

 **主題單字心智圖** MP3 060 ▶

lonely /ˈləʊnli/ *adj.* 寂寞

I feel lonely when I study abroad without my family.
當我離開我的家人在國外讀書的時候，我覺得很寂寞。

nervous /ˈnɜː(r)vəs/ *adj.* 緊張的

When I make a speech in public, I feel so nervous.
當我在大眾面前演講，我覺得很緊張。

join /dʒɔɪn/ *v.* 參加

I am going to join a basketball team.
我要去參加籃球隊。

look forward to *v.* 期待

I am looking forward
to traveling to America.
我很期待去美國旅行。

move /muːv/ *v.* 搬家

I am going to move to Taipei next week.
我下周要搬去台北。

The Power of Believing
相信的力量

🍊 帶著寶貝一起讀

　　你想看到聖誕老人嗎？你覺得有聖誕老人嗎？

　　相信的力量是很強大的，這種力量可以讓很多事成真，例如我們有信心可以贏得比賽，贏得比賽的機率就大增，例如相信聖誕老人會送你禮物，「相信」讓自己的生活保有活力與想像。但更難能可貴的是對「自己可以辦到」的相信，如果能有這種強烈的相信，那麼你的內心會變堅強，即使遇到挫折，也能在短的時間內爬起來，繼續向前，因為知道自己只是「還沒」達到而已。試試相信的力量吧！一定會給你的生命帶來魔法。

Parents

Grandparents

There's a boy who doesn't **believe** in Christmas, and he also spreads his **doubt**s to his sister. On Christmas Eve, with a firm doubt, he goes to bed. Suddenly he finds a train waiting in front of his house. The train is bound for the North Pole, where Santa Claus lives. He has some doubts at first, but eventually the boy boards the train. On the train, he meets other children. Among them, there is a girl and a boy who doesn't believe in Christmas either. When the train arrives at the North Pole, the three accidentally takes a **journey** without the rest of the people and end up in the gift sorting room. The girl leads the two boys with a strong belief on their way to reuniting with the rest of the people and to seeing Santa.

Everyone is cheering and dancing to the sound of the **bell**s on the reindeer's harness before Sata enters. However, the boy appears to be the only one who cannot hear the ringing bells. He finds a bell that falls off from the harness and shakes it. All he can hear is a sound that calls him a doubter and he finally whispers to himself that he believes. He shakes the bell again, and this time he can hear it ring. The boy meets Santa Claus.

Santa gives him the bell as his first gift. After a series of **magical** events, the boy discovers that there are wonders in life as long as he believes. Even after he has grown up, he can still hear the sound of the bell.

　　有個不相信聖誕節的男孩，而他也告訴他的妹妹不要相信有聖誕老人。在聖誕夜晚，抱著堅定的懷疑，他上床睡覺。突然他發現一台火車停在房子前方，正要前往聖誕老人居住的北極。他一開始不是很確定，但最後還是上了火車。在火車上，他遇到了其他的小孩。其中一位是個小女孩，另一位是一個叫比利（Billy）的男生，他也不相信聖誕節。當火車到達北極的時候，三個人意外的獨自展開一趟冒險旅程，最後來到禮物分配室。女孩全程藉著自己強烈的信仰帶領他們，出發回到隊伍中以及目睹聖誕老人。

　　大家都在向著麋鹿身上的鈴鐺聲歡呼與跳舞，但男孩似乎是唯一一位聽不到鈴鐺聲的人。他後來發現了一顆掉下來的鈴鐺，搖了一搖，只聽到叫他「懷疑者」的聲音，他最終低聲跟自己說「我相信」。他再試著搖了一次鈴鐺，這次他可以聽到鈴鐺聲了。男孩看到了聖誕老人，聖誕老人把鈴鐺給他，當做第一份禮物。在一系列的神奇事件之後，男孩了解到，只要自己相信，生命終究會充滿驚奇。即使他長大之後，他依然可以聽到鈴鐺聲。

 故事單字一起學　MP3 062 ▶

❶ believe /bɪ`liv/ *v.* 相信
I can't believe you're leaving.
我無法相信你已經要離開了。

❷ doubt /daʊt/ *n.* 懷疑
I have no doubt that you will do well.
我很確信你可以做得很好。

❸ journey /`dʒɝnɪ/ *n.* 旅行
Life is like a journey.
人生就像一趟旅程。

❹ bell /bɛl/ *n.* 鈴鐺
Ring the bell when you arrive.
你到的時候按電鈴。

❺ magical /`mædʒɪkl̩/ *adj.* 有魔力的
Camping under the stars is a magical experience.
在星空下露營是個有魔力的經驗。

一句一句練習說　MP3 063 ▶

What do you believe in? 你相信什麼？

Communication

❶ I believe in unicorns.
我相信有獨角獸。

❷ I believe in Tooth Fairy.
我相信有牙仙子。

❸ I believe in magic.
我相信魔法。

❹ I believe in science.
我相信科學。

❺ I believe in art.
我相信藝術。

 主題單字心智圖　MP3 064 ▶

Tooth Fairy /ˈtuθ ˌfɛrɪ/ *n.* 牙仙子

I left my tooth for Tooth Fairy.
我把我的牙齒留給了牙仙子。

science /ˈsaɪəns/ *n.* 科學

Science is my favorite subject.
科學是我最喜歡的科目。

unicorn /ˈjunɪ ˌkɔrn/ *n.* 獨角獸

Do unicorns exist?
世上有獨角獸嗎？

magic /ˈmædʒɪk/ *n.* 魔術、魔法

She uses her magic to move things around.
她用她的魔法移動東西。

art /ɑrt/ *n.* 藝術

You can see the most famous art works in the art museum.
在美術館你可以看到最有名的藝術品。

Don't Judge A Book by Its Cover
不以貌取人

🍋 **帶著寶貝一起讀**

　　我們有時候會因為一個人的外貌或是因為一件事，例如同學的外表髒髒的，或是這個人不小心撞了你，就不喜歡這個人。但如果我們有機會好好跟這個人相處，很多時候我們會發現，其實這個人沒有我們想像的那麼糟糕，甚至可以和我們成為好朋友。所以我們千萬不要「judge a book by its cover」，要深入了解之後再下判斷喔。你有沒有這個經驗呢？說說看吧！一開始你對這個人的感覺是什麼呢？後來你為什麼接受他了呢？

Parents

Grandparents

Shrek is an ogre who keeps other creatures out and lives **alone**. His peaceful days quickly ended by Lord Farquaad, who throws all fairy tale figures into his **swamp** and among them is a talking Donkey. To get his swamp back, he agrees to fight a dragon and rescue Princess Fiona, someone that Lord Farquaad wants to marry. Donkey leads the way. After Shrek and Donkey successfully rescue Princess Fiona, they rest and spend the night on a cliff. That night, Donkey asks about why Shrek likes being alone. Shrek tells Donkey that the problem is how people always judge him before they **know** him.

The next morning, they set off. On their way, Shrek realizes that Princess Fiona isn't just a regular princess and she is different from what he thinks. She burps in front of others and she can fight. She also solves problems for Shrek and Donkey. Shrek falls in love with Princess Fiona. Even though at first Princess Fiona is shocked by Shrek's appearance, she slowly falls for Shrek as well. One night, Donkey finds out that Fiona is cursed and will turn into an ogress at night. He tells Fiona to reveal the truth to Shrek since they are in love with each other.

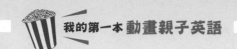
The two are finally in each other's arms and Shrek gives Fiona a **true** love's kiss which breaks the curse but makes Fiona an ogress forever. Although Fiona is a bit troubled by not being **beautiful**, she is beautiful in Shrek's eyes. They finally get married with everyone's blessing.

　　史瑞克（Shrek）是一隻怪物，他遠離其他生物並獨居。他平靜的日子很快就被法克大人（Lord Farquaad）給打斷了，法克大人把全部的童話故事角色都趕到史瑞克的沼澤，而其中一隻是會講話的驢子（Donkey）。為了把沼澤拿回來，他同意去打敗火龍，救出法克大人想娶的費歐娜公主（Princess Fiona），而驢子負責帶路。在史瑞克和驢子成功救出費歐娜公主之後，他們中途休息，並在懸崖上過了一晚。那天晚上，驢子問史瑞克為什麼他喜歡自己一個人，史瑞克告訴驢子，問題出在人們總是在認識他之前就評斷他。隔天早上，他們出發在路上時，史瑞克發現費歐娜公主不像一般的公主，和自己想像的很不同，費歐娜公主在人面前打嗝，而且會打架，還會幫史瑞克和驢子解決問題。史瑞克愛上了費歐娜公主，而雖然費歐娜公主一開始被史瑞克的外表嚇到，也漸漸愛上史瑞克。有一天晚上，驢子發現費歐娜公主被詛咒了，晚上就會變成怪物。驢子建議費歐納公主要告訴史瑞克，因為他們彼此相愛。最終史瑞克和費歐娜相擁彼此入懷，史瑞克給了費歐娜真愛之吻，因此打破了詛咒，但費歐娜卻永遠變成了怪物。雖然費歐娜對於自己不再美麗覺得有點煩惱，不過在史瑞克的眼裡，費歐娜是最美麗的。他們最終在大家的祝福之下舉行婚禮。

 故事單字一起學　MP3 066 ▶

1 alone /əˈloʊn/ *adj.* 單獨的
Please leave me alone for a while.
請讓我一個人靜一靜一會兒。

2 swamp /swɑmp/ *n.* 沼澤
Some frogs live in the swamp.
有一些青蛙住在沼澤裡。

3 know /no/ *v.* 知道
Don't you know that she loves you?
難道你不知道她愛你嗎？

4 true /tru/ *adj.* 真實的
Is it true that he's back?
他真的回來了嗎？

5 beautiful /ˈbjutəfəl/ *adj.* 美麗的
It's such a beautiful day.
今天真是太美好了。

一句一句練習說　MP3 067 ▶

What kind of topics can you talk about when you meet new friends?
第一次見到新朋友可以聊什麼呢？

Communication

❶ It's nice to meet you.
很高興認識你。

❷ What do you do in your free time?
你空閒時間都做什麼呢？

❸ Where did you get this beautiful bag?
你在哪裡買到這麼漂亮的袋子呢？

❹ When is your birthday?
你的生日是什麼時候呢？

❺ Who is your favorite singer?
你最喜歡的歌手是誰呢？

 主題單字心智圖　MP3 068 ▶

free time /fri taɪm/ *n.* 空閒時間

I watch movies in my free time.
我有空的時候都看電影。

nice /naɪs/ *adj.* 美好的

It's very nice of you to say.
你這樣說，我很開心。

beautiful /ˈbjutəfəl/ *adj.* 美麗的

She gave birth to a beautiful girl.
她生了一個美麗的女兒。

favorite /ˈfevərɪt/ *adj.* 最喜歡的

This is my favorite restaurant.
這是我最喜歡的餐廳。

birthday /ˈbɝθˌde/ *n.* 生日

She bought a dress as her own birthday present.
她為自己買了一件洋裝作為自己的生日禮物。

No One Is Perfect
不完美也沒關係

🎞 帶著寶貝一起讀

你想要改變自己哪個地方嗎？為什麼會想改變呢？

每個人都想要完美，但事實是沒有人可以做到永遠 100 分。我們都有一些自己或是同學、朋友無法忍受的特質，當然，我們可以適時調整成自己和旁人都舒服的狀態，但我們也不能一昧將自己變成旁人想要的樣子。最重要的，我們要先接受全部的自己，才有機會讓周遭的人真正進入你的心。千萬不要太擔心，真正的朋友會一直在你身邊，無論如何都會愛著你。

Parents

Grandparents

主題小劇場　MP3 069 ▶

Dory is a **forgetful** fish who suffers from short-term memory loss. When she was little, she separated from her parents. She looks for her parents for a very long time but always fails because she can't remember a thing. Afterwards, she bumps into Marlin, who is looking for his son, Nemo. After she helps Marlin find Nemo, she lives with Marlin and Nemo. One day she goes on a field trip with Nemo and remembers something from her childhood. Then she decides to look for her family. On their way, Dory accidentally gets Nemo hurt, after which Marlin snaps at her about her forgetfulness. She feels hurt and swims off, trying to get some help. She ends up in the Marine Life Institute. Inside the institute, Dory remembers more and also gets to meet many other ocean animals. Some of them have **problems**, just like her. Dory finally finds her childhood home but her parents are nowhere to be found. She gets some clues and goes through some pipes to find her parents. After many difficulties, she falls into the sea alone. She panics because of her short-term memory; she is not confident in herself and think she always needs people's help to a place, but she quickly calms herself down. Then she finds shells in her childhood memory, and following them, she finds her parents and reunites with them. Dory is **fearless** after this adventure now because she finally knows that even with some **shortcoming**s, her parents and her friends love her and that she can still do things well **on her own**.

多莉（Dory）是隻健忘的魚，她患有短期記憶喪失症。她小時候不小心和父母走失了。她花了很多時間找她的父母，但一直失敗因為她的的記憶力太差了。之後，她碰上在找兒子尼莫（Nemo）的馬林（Marlin），在幫馬林找回尼莫之後，他們便住在一起。有一天，多莉和尼莫一起參加了校外教學，她突然有了一些兒時的記憶，她決定去尋找她的家人。在路上，多莉不小心害尼莫受了傷，馬林非常的生氣，責備了多莉的健忘。多莉內心很受傷，但游開想找人來幫忙，最後卻跑進海洋生物研究所。

在研究所裡，多莉想起了更多事，也遇到其他海洋生物，其中一些也和多莉一樣有些問題。多莉終於找到他童年時的家，但還是卻找不到父母，但她得到一些線索，所以游過管子繼續尋找她的父母。經過重重困難，最後她獨自掉進大海中。她很慌張，因為她的短期失意症，她對自己沒有信心，而且認為自己總是需要別人的幫忙。她一直覺得自己沒有別人的幫忙，無法到達目的地，但她很快冷靜下來。她觀察四周，發現了一些出現在她童年記憶的貝殼，一路沿著它們，她找到並和父母團員。經過這一次的冒險，她變得無所畏懼，因為她終於了解到雖然有一些缺點，但是她的父母和朋友都還是愛著這樣的她，而且她也是一條能獨當一面的魚。

 **故事單字一起學** MP3 070 ▶

❶ **forgetful** /fɚ`gɛtfəl/ *adj.* 健忘的
She becomes forgetful as she grows older.
隨著年紀變大，她也變得健忘。

❷ **problem** /`prɑbləm/ *n.* 問題
We will help you solve the problem.
我們會幫忙你解決問題。

❸ **fearless** /`fɪrlɪs/ *adj.* 大膽的
She is a fearless hiker.
她是位勇敢的徒步旅行者。

❹ **shortcoming** /`ʃɔrt,kʌmɪŋ/ *n.* 缺點
I am aware of my own shortcomings.
我很清楚我的缺點是什麼。

❺ **on one's own** /ɑn wʌns on/ *ph.* 獨自
She travels around the world on her own.
她一個人環遊世界。

How do you encourage people who can't do well?
你怎麼鼓勵失敗的人？

Communication

❶ Don't judge yourself.
不要批評自己。

❷ Take a deep breath.
深呼吸。

❸ Don't quit.
不要放棄。

❹ You can always try again.
你可以不斷嘗試。

❺ Relax and see what is problem first.
放輕鬆然後先看看問題是什麼。

主題單字心智圖　MP3 072 ▶

encourage /ɪnˋkɝɪdʒ/ *v.* 鼓勵
My father encouraged me to learn English.
我的父親鼓勵我去學英語。

quit /kwɪt/ *v.* 放棄
Winners never quit and quitters never win.
勝利者從不放棄，
而半途而廢者絕對無法成功。

judge /dʒʌdʒ/ *v.* 評判
We shouldn't judge people harshly.
我們不該嚴厲的評斷別人。

again /əˋgɛn/ *adv.* 再一次
Let's watch that movie again.
我們再看一次那部電影。

breath /brɛθ/ *v.* 呼吸
I tried to hold my breath under water.
我試著在水中憋氣。

PART 2

Let's Learn More
更上一層樓

Unit 19 大英雄天團 Big Hero 6
Leave Behind Your Hatred
放下仇恨

🎬 帶著寶貝一起讀

　　如果同學做出讓你很生氣的事情，你會怎麼做呢？

　　我們會有非常生氣的時候，可能是很生氣兄弟姊妹拿我們的東西，或是不開心同學說我們的壞話。這時候，我們會想要報仇，讓他們也跟我們感覺一樣生氣，生氣是正常的，不過如果我們靜下來想一想，我們做了一樣的事情，報復他們之後，感覺並沒有比較好，而且事情也沒有得到解決。假如我們從不同的角度看這件事情，換另一個方法，一起解決，一定會有更美好的結果。想想生活中的例子，一起討論看看可以怎麼做吧！

Parents

Grandparents

主題小劇場　　MP3 073 ▶

Hiro is a boy who is into street bot-fights and doesn't want to continue school. His brother, Tadashi, tries to change his mind and convince Hiro to enter his school, San Fransokyo Institute of Technology. He comes up with an amazing invention, micro-bots and he does impress all in the student showcase. Unfortunately, on the same night, Hiro loses his brother, as well as his invention in a fire at the showcase. Feeling **depressed** about losing his brother, Hiro refused to step out of his room and is surprised by his brother's robot, Baymax, and a piece of his micro-bots. Baymax leads him to the rest of his micro-bots and a masked man who has stolen Hiro's micro-bot technology. In order to take back his micro-bots, he upgrades his brother's invention and **comes up with** special suits for them.

The group comes to an island to find the masked man. When Hiro takes the mask off the man, he discovers that Tadashi's professor is behind all this. Hiro gets really mad and turns Baymax into a killing machine and tells Baymax to kill the professor. His brother's friends stop this in time. Later, Baymax helps Hiro see that **revenge** is not going to change anything and his brother won't want him to get revenge and use the robot to kill people. Hiro grows up and learns to look at things from different **angles.** Now he has his own new life with his superhero friends. Together they are six superheroes that save people **in need**.

　　濱田廣（Hiro）是個熱愛街頭機器人戰鬥和沒有繼續學業的男孩。他的哥哥濱田正（Tadashi）試著想改變他的想法，說服他進入自己就讀的舊金山科技學院。濱田廣（Hiro）發明出很棒的微型機器人，讓學生展覽上的所有人印象深刻。不幸地，因為學生展上的大火，他在同一個晚上失去了他的哥哥和自己的發明。他失去哥哥後非常的憂鬱，足不出戶，卻被哥哥發明的機器人杯麵（Baymax）嚇一跳，還發現自己微型機器人的一小部分。杯麵帶他找到了他剩下的微型機器人以及一位蒙面男子，男子偷了他的微型機器人。為了拿回自己的微型機器人，他將哥哥的機器人升級並找了哥哥的朋友來幫他，也幫他們做了特別的戰鬥服。

　　這群人一起來到一座小島找這位蒙面男子。當濱田廣拿掉男子的面具時，他發現原來這一切都是哥哥的教授在搞怪，濱田廣非常的生氣，把杯麵變成一個殺人機器，要杯麵把教授殺了，哥哥的朋友及時阻止一切。不久後，杯麵幫助濱田廣了解到，報仇並不能改變什麼，而且他的哥哥也不會希望他報仇，用機器人殺人。濱田廣長大了並學會從不同的角度看事情。他和他的超級英雄朋友開始了屬於自己的新生活他們現在是六位英雄，專門幫助有需要的人。

 故事單字一起學　MP3 074 ▶

❶ **come up with** /kʌm ʌp wɪð/ *ph.* 想出
We need to come up with a new idea.
我們需要想出一個新方法。

❷ **depressed** /dɪ`prɛst/ *adj.* 憂鬱的
He is depressed because of his scores.
他因為成績感到很憂鬱。

❸ **revenge** /rɪ`vɛndʒ/ *n.* 復仇
He wants to get revenge for his broken heart.
他想為自己的心碎報仇。

❹ **angle** /ˋæŋgl/ *n.* 角度
We can solve the problem from a different angle.
我們可以從另一個角度解決這個問題。

❺ **in need** /ɪn nid/ *ph.* 有需求的
Let's help a friend in need.
我們一起幫忙有需要的朋友吧。

一句一句練習說　MP3 075 ▶

How do I deal with my anger?
我生氣的時候怎麼辦？

Communication

❶ I know it's normal to feel angry.
我知道感到生氣是正常的。

❷ I tell myself to relax.
我告訴我自己放鬆。

❸ I find out why I feel angry.
我會找出讓我生氣的原因。

❹ I won't hurt people or animals.
我不會傷害人或小動物。

❺ I tell my friends I feel upset and angry.
我會告訴我的朋友我感到沮喪和生氣。

 主題單字心智圖 MP3 076 ▶

anger /ˈæŋgɚ/ *n.* 怒氣

She yelled at her brother with anger.
她很生氣的對弟弟大叫。

deal with /dil wɪð/ *ph.* 處理

I can deal with my own problems.
我可以處理自己的問題。

relax /rɪˈlæks/ *v.* 放鬆

I read books to relax.
我看書來放鬆。

hurt /hɝt/ *v.* 傷害

I will not let him hurt you.
我不會讓他傷害你的。

practice /ˈpræktɪs/ *v.* 練習

She practices piano every night.
她每個晚上練習鋼琴。

131

Unit 20 可可夜總會Coco

The Value Of Family Ties
家庭關係的重要

帶著寶貝一起讀

　　你和家人會吵架嗎？你們會有意見不合的時候嗎？你跟家人天天相處在一起，但是有時候還是會和家人有意見不合和吵架的時候，這時候絕對不能衝動「離家出走」或做出傷害彼此的事情。和家人吵架的時候，絕對要學會好好溝通，說出各自的想法，練習不要急著發脾氣。電影中的米高和家人賭氣吵架，意見不合後離家，經過一連串的冒險之後，他終於了解到家人的用心，在過程中家人也終於願意理解並尊重他，他們都學到寶貴的一課，因為愛你的人永遠會在你的身旁支持你，擔心你也為你加油。

Parents

Grandparents

MP3 077 ▶

On the Day of the Dead, Mexican family put on their beloved and dead family photos to lead their family members to come back from the dead world to the living world. Miguel lives in a big Mexican **family**. The story begins on the Day of the Dead. Miguel loves music but it is banned in his family. He finds a torn **picture** and thinks his great-great-grandfather is the dead superstar, Ernesto de la Cruz. One day, Miguel fights with his family for music again and runs away because they smashed his guitar. He tries to steal Ernesto's guitar but accidentally goes into the dead world. In the world of the dead, he was told he has to get his family **member**'s blessings before the sun rises to return to the land of the living.

He decides to meet Ernesto for a blessing. One his way, he meets Hector, a ghost who is disappearing because none of his family put his photos. Only his daughter can **remember** him but she is losing her **memory**. Hector promises to take Miguel to Ernesto. In return, Miguel has to bring Hector's photo to the world of the living. Later he finds out that Hector is his real great-great-grandfather and that evil Ernesto killed Hector. In the end,

Miguel almost is running out of time. Hector gives Miguel his blessings and all of Miguel's dead family helps him without any conditions. Miguel finally goes back to the living world. After this adventure Miguel regrets running from family because of an immature decision. He now learns that family always supports and protects him because his family loves him forever.

　　在亡靈節（the Day of the Dead）這一天，墨西哥家庭會放上他們逝去親愛家人的照片引領他們的家人從亡靈的世界回來。米高（Miguel）住在墨西哥的一個大家庭裡。他熱愛音樂，但他的家庭禁止任何人玩音樂。有一天米高發現一張被撕破的照片，他認為他的曾曾祖父就是有名的已故大明星，安尼斯托‧德拉古司（Ernesto de la Cruz）。有一天，米高又因為音樂跟家人吵架，他們摔壞他的吉他，他因此離家出走。他跑去想偷德拉古司的吉他，不小心進入了亡靈的世界。而他必須在日出之前得到已故親人的祝福，才能回到活人的世界。米糕決定找德拉古司祝福他，途中他遇到埃克托（Hector），一個快消失的鬼魂，沒有家人放上他的照片，因為除了他的女兒，沒有人記得他，可惜是他女兒的記憶也慢慢流失了。埃克托答應要帶米高去見德拉古司，而米高必須要把埃克托的照片帶回人間。最後米高發現埃克托才是自己真正的曾曾祖父，是邪惡的德拉古司殺了埃克托。最後米高差點沒時間了，是海特無條件地給他祝福和其他已故親人的幫助下回到他的世界。在這次冒險之後，他後悔自己因為一個不成熟的決定而離開家人，他現在知道家人會永遠支持和保護他，因為他們會永遠愛他。

 故事單字一起學　MP3 078 ▶

① **family** /ˈfæməlɪ/ *n.* 家庭、家人
She grows up in a large family.
她在一個大家庭長大。

② **picture** /ˈpɪktʃɚ/ *n.* 照片
I take a lot of pictures when I travel.
我旅遊都拍很多照片。

③ **member** /ˈmɛmbɚ/ *n.* 成員
Grandfather is the oldest family member.
祖父是年紀最長的家族成員。

④ **remember** /rɪˈmɛmbɚ/ *v.* 記得
I remember reading that story.
我記得有念過那個故事。

⑤ **memory** /ˈmɛmərɪ/ *n.* 記憶
Christmas brings me wonderful memories.
聖誕節帶給我美好的回憶。

一句一句練習說　MP3 079 ▶

How to show your love to your Mom and Dad?

你如何表現對爸爸和媽媽的愛呢？

Communication

❶ I hug my parents every day.
我每天抱我的爸媽。

❷ We often call each other.
我們時常通電話。

❸ We have family meals every night.
我們每天晚上一起吃飯。

❹ We celebrate Chinese New Year together every year.
我們每年一起慶祝農曆新年。

❺ We always go camping together on the weekend. It's our tradition.
我們常常周末一起去露營。這是我們的傳統。

 主題單字心智圖　MP3 080 ▶

call /kɔl/ *v.* 撥打（電話）

I'll call you tonight.
我今天晚上會打電話給你。

meal /mil/ *n.* 一餐

We always have three meals a day.
我們都一天吃三餐。

hug /hʌg/ *v.* 擁抱

They hugged each other.
他們互相擁抱。

celebrate /ˋsɛləˌbret/ *v.* 慶祝

I'm going to celebrate my birthday with my family.
我要跟家人一起慶祝我的生日。

tradition /trəˋdɪʃən/ *n.* 傳統

We will make this as family tradition.
我們把這個當作家族傳統吧。

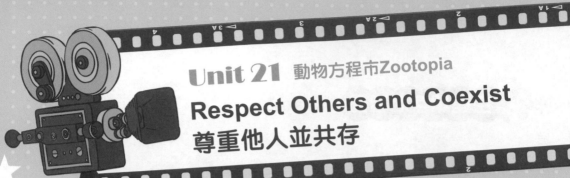

Unit 21 動物方程市Zootopia
Respect Others and Coexist
尊重他人並共存

帶著寶貝一起讀

　　你有沒有同學跟你很不一樣？和你喜歡不同的東西、聊不同的事物。我們剛認識新同學的時候，因為有些同學看起來和我們很不一樣，或是他們喜歡不同的東西，而不跟他們做朋友，甚至偷偷討厭他們。如果我們試著多了解他們，我們也許會發現彼此很多共同點，學著尊重對方，也可能會和從沒想過的人成為好朋友，就像電影裡面，兔子和狐狸變成好朋友，因為他們相處後，開始互相了解，然後一起合作讓世界變得更美好。

Parents

Grandparents

 主題小劇場　MP3 081 ▶

There is a world where all animals, **predators** or **prey**, live together. Judy Hopps is a 9-year-old bunny. She dreams of becoming a police officer and changing the world. Years later, after hard training, she becomes the first **bunny** officer in Zootopia because nobody thinks a bunny can become a police officer. One day, an otter disappears and his wife is looking for him. Judy helps her and asks a **fox**, Nick's help because he knows many animals. They follow clues and find the otter and other missing animals. They are locked in cages because they go crazy and attack other animals. The world knows about these locked animals. Judy tells reporters that all of these animals are predators and prey need to be more careful. Now all prey are worried and think all predators are scary. This hurts Nick's feelings as well because he thinks Judy doesn't trust him because he is a predator.

The distrust between prey and predators continues; and Judy thinks it's all her fault. Feeling sad, Judy returns to her hometown but finds out that it is a kind of flower that is making animals go crazy. Judy and Nick work together again. They find out a sheep is behind everything. The sheep used some tricks to make prey and predators against each other. Together, Judy and Nick have the sheep caught. Judy realizes that although all animals are different in appearance. They still can create an equal environment when they try to put themselves into others' shoes.

在這個世界裡，不管是獵食動物或獵物，所有的動物都住在一起。哈茱蒂（Judy Hopps）是一隻九歲的小兔子。她夢想成為一個警察，並改變這個世界。多年過後，經過辛苦的訓練，她終於成為動物方城市（Zootopia）的第一位兔子警察，因為沒有人相信兔子可以成為一個警察。有一天，有一隻水獺不見了，他的太太在找他。茱蒂幫忙她並請狐狸尼克（Nick）幫忙，因為尼克認識許多動物。他們跟著線索找到了水獺和其他動物，這些動物因為發瘋攻擊其他動物，都被關在籠子裡。後來大家都聽說有這些被關起來的動物，而茱蒂告訴記者這些動物都是獵食動物，要其他動物小心。因此所有的獵物都很擔心，也覺得獵食動物很恐怖，這也傷到了尼克的心，他認為茱蒂還是不相信他，因為他是一隻獵食動物。

獵食動物或獵物之間還是不信任對方，而茱蒂覺得這一切都是她的錯。茱蒂很傷心，回到她的家鄉，但後來發現讓獵食動物發瘋的是一種花。茱蒂和尼克，兩個人又一起合作他們發現原來是一隻羊在背後作怪，他利用一些技巧讓獵物和獵食動物反目，茱蒂和尼克合作，羊終於被逮捕了。茱蒂了解到，每隻動物的外表都不同，但如果他們願意站在對方的立場為對方著想，他們可以一起創造一個更平等的環境。

 故事單字一起學　MP3 082 ▶

1 **predator** /ˋprɛdətɚ/ *n.* 掠食性動物
Lions are predators.
獅子會獵食其他動物。

2 **prey** /pre/ *n.* 獵物
Zebras are prey to lions.
斑馬是獅子的獵物。

3 **bunny** /ˋbʌnɪ/ *n.* 小兔子
There are some cute bunnies in my house.
我家有一些可愛的小兔子。

4 **fox** /fɑks/ *n.* 狐狸
Foxes prey on rabbits.
狐狸會獵食兔子。

5 **understand** /ʌndɚˋstænd/ *v.* 了解、懂
I cannot understand the teacher.
我聽不懂老師在說什麼。

一句一句練習說　MP3 083 ▶

@#$%^

How do we show our respect?
我們如何表現尊重呢？

Communication

❶ Listen to people.
多聽別人說話。

❷ Don't yell at people.
不對人大聲說話。

❸ Don't tease people.
不隨便取笑別人。

❹ Let people make their own decision.
讓人自己做決定。

❺ Say you're sorry when you make a mistake.
當你犯錯時，要記的道歉。

 主題單字心智圖　MP3 084 ▶

respect /rɪˋspɛkt/ v. 尊重

I don't understand it, but I respect it.
我不了解它，但我尊重它。

yell /jɛl/ v. 喊叫

Stop yelling at me!
不要再對我那麼大聲說話！

tease /tiz/ v. 取笑、戲弄

My brother used to tease about my

red hair when we were little kids.
當我們還小時，我的哥哥總喜歡嘲笑我的紅髮。

sorry /ˋsɔrɪ/ adj. 感到抱歉的

I'm sorry I'm late.
遲到了很抱歉。

decision /dɪˋsɪʒ.ən/ n. 決定

She has to make some decision

about school chhosing.
她需要做一個關於選擇學校的決定。

143

帶著寶貝一起讀

　　當我們到一個沒去過的地方，見到外國人，常常會在認識他們之前，就先覺得這個地方或這個人應該是怎樣的，這是一種「偏見」，如果我們不小心的話，偏見很可能會傷害到自己或別人，一直以來有很多悲劇就是這樣造成的。雖然這部動畫的內容和歷史事實不一樣，鼓勵大家也去找找真的故事！但電影也提醒我們，即使大腦習慣有偏見，還是要告訴自己，記得放開心胸認識這個地方或聽聽對方的故事，就能像電影一樣，有個美好且和平的結局。

Parents　　**Grandparents**

主題小劇場　　MP3 085 ▶

A group of white people from London sail to a new land they haven't been to before. They plan to **take over** the land for gold. Among them is Captain John Smith. He leaves his people to **explore** the land alone. In the forest, he meets Pocahontas. Pocahontas is a Native American woman who lives on the land. John Smith and Pocahontas spend some time to get to know each other's **culture**. John Smith tells Pocahontas that they are here to give them better life which makes Pocahontas feels angry because these people from London look down on them. She tells John Smith that he only sees the surface. She shows him how much she and her people know about nature.

At the same time, John Smith's people and Pocahontas's people start their first small fight. Pocahontas and John Smith want to stop their people from **fight**ing and try to have the two sides to talk. However, none of their people think the other side can be trusted and they have no choice but to fight. Later they even start a war between the two sides because Pocahontas's people find she is John Smith's friend. The situation is getting

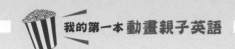
worse so Pocahontas tells her father, the chief to stop this and see how hatred hurt them. Finally her father listens to his **heart** and decides that his daughter is right. He should not let anger control him. In the end, the two sides make peace and learn to respect their differences.

　　一群來自英國的白人航行來到一片他們從未到過的新土地，他們計劃佔領土地，取得黃金，在他們之中是船長約翰‧史密斯（John Smith），他離開她的人們，自己一個人探索這片土地。在叢林裡，他遇見了寶嘉康蒂（Pocahontas），寶嘉康蒂是住在這片土地上的美洲原住民。史密斯和寶嘉康蒂花了一點時間了解對方的文化，史密斯告訴寶嘉康蒂他們是來改善寶嘉康蒂和她的人民的生活，這樣的話讓寶嘉康蒂很生氣，因為這些英國來的人看不起自己和人民，她告訴史密斯他只看到表面，她讓史密斯知道她和她的人民對大自然的了解。

　　這時候史密斯和寶嘉康蒂的人民起了第一次小衝突，寶嘉康蒂和史密斯想阻止雙方開打，並試著想讓雙方溝通，然而他們一點都不信任對方，兩邊都覺得打仗是唯一的選擇。這時候史密斯和寶嘉康蒂的人民開啟了第一場小衝突，寶嘉康蒂和史密斯想阻止雙方開打，並嘗試想讓雙方對話，然而沒人想要信任對方，兩邊都覺得打仗是唯一的選擇。那天晚上，寶嘉康蒂的人民發現她和史密斯是朋友，事情越演越烈，寶嘉康蒂請他的酋長父親看清仇恨對他們造成的影響，寶嘉康蒂的父親聆聽了自己的心，他知道寶嘉康蒂是對的，他不該讓憤怒控制自己，最後雙方維持和平並學著尊重彼此的不同。

 MP3 086 ▶

1 **take over** /tek `ovɚ/ *ph.* 接管
We need to come up with a new idea.
我們需要想出一個新點子。

- -

2 **explore** /ɪk`splor/ *v.* 探索
I will take them to explore the city.
我會帶著他們探索這個城市。

- -

3 **culture** /`kʌltʃɚ/ *n.* 文化
I like learning about new cultures.
我喜歡認識新文化。

- -

4 **fight** /faɪt/ *v.* 打架
You are fighting over nothing.
你們在為了一件小事打架。

- -

5 **heart** /hɑrt/ *n.* 心
Grandma Willow says to listen with your heart.
柳樹婆婆說要用心聆聽。

一句一句練習說 MP3 087 ▶

How do you learn about a culture?
你該如何認識一個文化?

Communication

❶ French kiss friends' cheek when they greet each other.

當法國人打招呼時,他們會親吻對方的臉頰。

❷ Chinese will give children red envelops in Chinese New Year.

中國人會在新年時給小孩子紅包。

❸ Playing soccer is German kids' favorite sports after school.

踢足球是德國小孩課後最喜歡的運動。

❹ Every country has different ways to celebrate New Year.

每一個國家有不同慶祝新年的方式。

❺ Asians will have many delicious foods in Chinese New Year.

亞洲人會在中國新年時享用許多美味的食物。

 主題單字心智圖 MP3 088 ▶

popular /ˈpɑpjələ/ *adj.* 流行的

He is the most popular singer in Taiwan.
他是台灣最受歡迎的歌手。

greet /grit/ *v.* 問候

We greet with a nod of the head.
我們會點頭打招呼。

country /ˈkʌntrɪ/ *n.* 國家

I have been to many countries.
我去過很多國家。

food /fud/ *n.* 食物

Food is the best way to know a culture.
食物是認識一個文化最好的方式。

sports /spɔrts/ *n.* 運動

Basketball is my favorite sport.
籃球是我最喜歡的運動。

Unit 23 功夫熊貓 Kung Fu Panda

When You Least Expect it
出乎意料之外

帶著寶貝一起讀

　　有時候你會遇過一個解決不了的問題，不管你怎麼努力都無法解決，因此你覺得很挫折難過，喪失信心。最好的方法是先不要太擔心，暫時把問題拋到一邊，冷靜下來，過一會兒，再回去看看自己的問題，也許就會在意外的地方找到答案喔！「功夫熊貓」中訓練阿波（Po）或打敗殘豹（Tai Lung）的方法都是出乎大家意料之外的喔！

Parents

Grandparents

 MP3 089 ▶

Po is a giant panda that lives in the valley. Grand **Master** Oogway, tells Master Shifu, a red panda, that his evil former student, Tai Lung, is going to return for revenge. They must select the Dragon Warrior to fight against Tai Lung. They hold a **match** to find the Dragon Warrior. Grand Master Oogway chooses Po as the Dragon Warrior. No one believes that Po can be the Dragon Warrior. Master Shifu has no choice but starts **training** Po, but the training doesn't work well in the beginning. When Po doubts himself, Master Oogway tells Po that he should focus on his training and be confident. Then Po and Master Shifu start to work hard and find the right way to improve him.

The next morning, Master Shifu finds Po in the kitchen eating because he is nervous. Master Shifu finds that Po can perform kung fu moves perfectly for foods. Now he knows that he can use food to train Po and turn him into a kung fu master. Po becomes very good at kung fu and earns the Dragon Scroll, which holds the **secret** to great power and only the Dragon Warrior can see. When Po opens the scroll, he sees nothing.

Later, Po can see himself in the scroll and understands that the secret to great power is belief in himself. Po faces Tai Lung and fights with Tai Lung in his own way. Different from what people **expect** at first, Po defeats Tai Lung and saves everyone in the valley.

阿波（Po）是一隻住在山谷中的大熊貓。龜大仙（Grand Master Oogway）告訴小熊貓師夫（Master Shifu）他以前的邪惡學生殘豹（Tai Lung）要回來復仇了，他們必須找到神龍大俠（Dragon Warrior）來對抗殘豹。他們舉辦一場比賽來找出神龍大俠。出乎意料之外，龜大仙選了阿波，並指定他為神龍大俠。沒人覺得阿波是神龍大俠，連師夫都不這樣覺得。師夫別無選擇，只好開始訓練阿波，一開始訓練進行的很不順利，當阿波開始懷疑自己，但龜大仙告訴阿波只要專注在訓練且對自己有信心。之後阿波和師父更努力的訓練，終於找到對的方法讓他進步─食物。

隔天早上，師夫發現阿波因為緊張在廚房吃東西，很多櫥櫃都被打破，而師夫發現阿波很多功夫招式都做得很好，現在他知道他可以利用食物訓練阿波。阿波的功夫變得很好，也贏得了神龍捲軸，捲軸裡藏了能獲得強大力量的秘密，這只有神龍大俠才能看。當阿波打開「神龍卷軸」後，裡面什麼也沒有。但阿波看到自己的倒影，他發現卷軸的秘密─相信自己就是最強的招式。當阿波面對殘豹時，他用自己的方式打敗殘暴。跌破眾人眼鏡，阿波打敗殘豹並且救了所有村民。

 故事單字一起學　MP3 090 ▶

❶ master /`mæstɚ/ *n.* 大師
People say he is the master of kung fu.
人們都說他是功夫大師。

❷ match /mætʃ/ *n.* 比賽
We won the match.
我們贏得這場比賽。

❸ train /tren/ *v.* 訓練
She is training for the next match.
她正為了下一場比賽受訓。

❹ secret /`sikrɪt/ *n.* 秘密
Please don't tell anyone my secret.
請不要把我的秘密告訴任何人。

❺ expect /ɪk`spɛkt/ *v.* 期待、預期
I didn't expect to see him so soon.
我沒想到會那麼快見到他。

一句一句練習說　MP3 091 ▶

How can I solve a problem?
我該怎麼解決問題？

Communication

❶ Don't worry. There must be different ways to solve the problems.
不用擔心。一定有很多解決問題的方法。

❷ Look up information online and books to solve the problem.
上網或是翻書找資料解決問題。

❸ Be creative.
運用創意。

❹ Calm down first.
先冷靜下來。

❺ Ask your friends and parents for help.
請朋友和父母幫你的忙。

主題單字心智圖　MP3 092 ▶

different /ˈdɪfərənt/ *adj.* 不同的
She is different from my other classmate.
她和我其他同學不一樣。

way /we/ *n.* 方法
I'll find a new way to solve the problem.
我會找出一個解決這個問題的新方法。

creative /krɪˈetɪv/ *adj.* 有創意的
My friend tells stories
in a very creative way.
我朋友用很有創意
的方式說故事。

calm down /kɑːm daʊn/ *ph.* 冷靜
Calm down and tell us what is going on.
冷靜下來告訴我們發生什麼事情了。

look up / lʊk ʌp/ *ph.* 搜尋
I didn't know the meaning of the word so I looked it up in the dictionary.
我不懂這個單字的意思，所以我翻字典查這個字。

帶著寶貝一起讀

　　你覺得學習是什麼呢？你喜歡學習嗎？學習對學生來說就是去上學，吸收課堂上的知識，國文、英文、數學和地理等科目。除了教室外，這個世界還有好多新事物等著我們去學習，學習不是只有成績和課本裡的知識，人生到處都有值得學習的事物。隨時保持一顆樂於學習的心，你的每一天將變得不一樣，生活更豐富，也許會有意料之外的事情發生喔！電影中的野獸，被魔咒困在城堡中很久，因為打開心房學習新事物，也贏得從沒期待過的愛，一起算算看你這個星期學了幾樣新東西吧！

Parents

Grandparents

A prince is turned into a **beast** because he doesn't know how to love but cares more about his appearance. To break the **spell**, he must learn to love someone from his heart and earn the person's love in return, or he will be the ugly beast forever. Belle is a girl who lives in a village with her father. She loves to read. Every time her Dad goes on a business trip, he brings a gift back to his beloved daughter, Belle. One day, Belle's father accidentally walks into the beast's castle for a rose as Belle's gift but he is locked up by the beast. Belle goes to the castle to save her father. She finds her weak father in the castle and asks to stay in the castle **instead of** her father. The beast lets Belle's father go and keeps Belle in the castle. When she is in the castle, she walks into the west wing, where the beast warns her to stay away from. While Belle is running away, she runs into a pack of wolves. The beast comes to save her and gets hurt badly. Even though Belle is afraid, she helps take the beast back to the castle and treats his wounds. The two become close and the beast becomes kinder. The beast decides to try his best to win Belle's love. He takes her into a room full of books. They read together and she teaches him to read. He changes. He also learns to eat with manners and be kind to other people and animals. The beast doesn't **stop** learning and that what matters is the **inner** beauty. He falls in love with Belle and gets her love in return. Finally, the spell is broken and the beast turns back into a handsome prince.

　　有位王子因為不懂得愛而被變成一隻野獸，如果想要破除魔咒，他必須學會真心愛人，並得到對方的愛。貝兒是個住在村莊裡的女孩，和其他女生不同的是她很愛閱讀。有一天，貝兒的父親不小心闖進野獸的城堡，被野獸關了起來。貝兒跑到城堡想救父親，在城堡裡她找到虛弱的父親，並跟野獸要求要代替父親留在城堡裡。野獸放走了貝兒的父親，並把貝兒留在城堡裡。當貝兒在城堡裡時，誤闖了野獸要她不要去的西廂，野獸非常的生氣，把貝兒給嚇跑了。

　　當貝兒在逃跑的時候，遇到了一群野狼，野獸前來拯救她，被傷得很嚴重。雖然貝兒還是很怕他，還是幫忙把野獸帶回城堡，並幫忙治療他的傷口。貝兒和野獸越來越親近，野獸也變得越來越善良。野獸想好好對待貝兒，並想了解貝兒的興趣，他帶貝兒去一間滿是書籍的房間，他們一起看書，貝兒也教野獸怎麼閱讀。野獸還學習餐桌禮儀，以及如何友善對待其他人和動物，野獸不停地學習，想贏得貝兒的歡心。慢慢的，野獸了解到，他不需要擔心自己的外表，內在美才是最重要的，他愛上了貝兒，而貝兒也愛上了野獸，魔咒終於被解除，野獸也變回帥氣的王子。

 MP3 094 ▶

❶ beast /bist/ *n.* 野獸
The lion is the kind of beasts。
獅子是萬獸之王。

❷ spell /spɛl/ *n.* 咒語
The witch cast a spell on the prince.
巫婆對王子下了咒語。

❸ instead of /ɪn`stɛd ɔv/ *ph.* 代替
I'll have rice instead of noodles.
我要吃飯而不吃麵。

❹ stop /stɑp/ *v.* 停止
You can't stop me from going.
你不能阻止我去。

❺ inner /`ɪnɚ/ *adj.* 裡面的
Inner beauty is more important than outer beauty.
內在美比外表更重要。

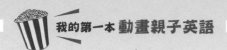
 一句一句練習說 MP3 095 ▶

How do you learn new things?
你怎麼學習新事物？

Communication

❶ I read a lot of books.
我看很多書。

❷ I join a club.
我可以參加社團。

❸ I take online classes.
我參加線上課程。

❹ I listen to the stories my grandparents tell me.
我聽我的祖父母講故事。

❺ I go abroad to travel.
我可以出國旅行。

主題單字心智圖　MP3 096 ▶

club /klʌb/ *n.* 社團
I am going to join the English club.
我要參加英語社。

book /bʊk/ *n.* 書籍
I try to finish one book every week.
我試著每週讀一本書。

online /ˈɑnˌlaɪn/ *adj.* 線上的
Now I can talk to my friends online.
我現在可以跟朋友在線上聊天。

abroad /əˈbrɔd/ *adj.* 在國外
She moved abroad five years ago.
她五年前搬到國外去。

class /klæs/ *n.* 課程
How many classes does he take?
他上幾堂課？

Unit 25 汽車總動員 Cars
Do The Right Thing
做對的事情

🎞 帶著寶貝一起讀

你有參加過比賽嗎?贏得比賽的感覺是什麼呢?

有時候我們太想要贏得比賽,會不小心做出違規或是傷害別人的事情,像路霸(Chick Hicks),只想要贏得比賽,沒有顧慮到自己和別人的安全,最後用傷害人的方法贏得比賽。而閃電麥坤(Lightning McQueen)一開始只想著要當最快的賽車,以為自己不需要別人的幫助,周遭的人都離他而去。有贏得比賽的熱忱是一件好事,但在我們拼命向勝利前進的同時,我們也要了解到有時候歡樂過程比勝利的結果更重要呢!

Parents

Grandparents

 主題小劇場 MP3 097 ▶

All cars are ready to **compete** with each other in a **race**. One of them is Chick Hicks. He has never won first place, but this year he is looking forward to **winning**. This is Lightning McQueen and this is his first year racing; he is doing really well. During the race, Chick Hicks keeps hitting other cars in order to win. This causes a lot of cars to crash into each other. Too **eager** to win, McQueen doesn't stop to change his tires. He keeps going until he burns two of his tires. He still makes it to the finish line, but his team is very angry and leaves because he is too proud and didn't take others' advice.

The race ends. It is a tie between three cars, including Lightning McQueen. They have to have another race in California. On his way to California, McQueen accidentally destroys a town's road because he wants to arrive in California earlier. He is forced to stay in the town and help fix everything. When he is in the town, he learns that the town isn't always as old as it looks now. No one visits the town now because people all want to be **fast** like him. However, the country is still waiting for Lightning McQueen and people come to find him. They take McQueen back to finish the race in California. With his friends'

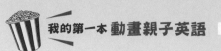

help, Lightning McQueen is about to win the race. Just then, a car is hit by Chick Hicks and is badly hurt. Lightning McQueen quits the race to help the car finish the game. McQueen doesn't win but everyone cheers for Lightning McQueen this time. Lightning McQueen finally understands that doing the right thing is more important than winning.

三部車準備好要在比賽中互相競爭，其中一部是路霸（Chick Hicks），他從沒得過第一名，但今年他很期待可以贏得比賽，另外還有閃電麥坤（Lightning McQueen），雖然這是他賽車的第一年，但他表現得非常好。在比賽過程中，路霸為了贏，不斷的撞其他的車，最後造成連環車禍。太想贏得比賽，麥坤完全不停下來換輪胎，他一直不斷繼續，直到他燒壞了自己的輪胎。他還是到達了終點，但他的團隊卻生氣地離開了。

比賽結束了，包含閃電麥坤的三台車平手，他們必須再到加州（California）比一場賽。再去加州的路上，麥坤因為想早點抵達，不小心毀掉了一個城鎮的道路。他被迫留下來幫忙修理一切。他在城鎮的期間，他聽說原來這個城鎮並不是一直都那麼老舊，現在沒人要來這裡，是因為大家都求快,就像他。然而，全國的人都還在等麥坤，跑來找他。人們把麥坤帶回去完成加州的比賽。有了城鎮朋友的幫忙，麥坤就快要贏得比賽了，就在這時候，有一台車被路霸給撞了，受了很嚴重的傷，麥坤決定放棄比賽，去幫忙這台車完成比賽，雖然他沒有贏得比賽但大家為麥坤歡呼。麥坤終於明白，做對的事情比贏得比賽更重要。

 故事單字一起學　MP3 098 ▶

1 **compete** /kəm`pit/ *v.* 競爭
She competes against her brother in matches.
她常在比賽裡跟自己的哥哥比賽。

- -

2 **race** /res/ *n.* 比賽
He just won the race.
他剛贏了比賽。

- -

3 **winning** /'wɪnɪŋ/ *n.* 勝利
Winning gives them more confidence.
這個勝利為他們帶來更多自信。

- -

4 **eager** /ˋigɚ/ *adj.* 急切的
She is eager for a fresh start.
她很急著要重新開始。

- -

5 **fast** /fæst/ *adj.* 快的
Time goes by too fast.
時間過得太快了。

一句一句練習說 MP3 099 ▶

@#$%^

Communication

What should a good kid do?
一個好孩子應該做什麼？

❶ Try to stay healthy.
保持健康。

❷ I should always tidy up my room.
我應該常常整理房間。

❸ It's important to be polite.
有禮貌是很重要的。

❹ You can try your best to help people.
你可以盡力幫助別人。

❺ Reduce, reuse, and recycle.
垃圾減量、重複使用、回收再利用。

主題單字心智圖 MP3 100 ▶

healthy /ˈhɛlθɪ/ *adj.* 健康的

It's not healthy to stay up all night.
整個晚上熬夜是不健康的。

vegetable /ˈvedʒtəb(ə)l/ *n.* 蔬菜

Eat more fresh fruit, vegetables, and salads.
多吃水果、蔬菜和沙拉。

reduce /rɪˈdjus/ *v.* 減少

We need to reduce waste.
我們需要減少垃圾。

polite /pəˈlaɪt/ *adj.* 有禮貌的

It's not polite to stare at people.
盯著人看是不禮貌的。

tidy up *ph.* 整理

Please tidy up the toys before you go to bed.
睡覺之前請整理一下玩具。

Beware Of The Green-Eyed Monster: Jealousy 小心綠眼怪獸：羨慕嫉妒

帶著寶貝一起讀

當你最好的朋友和別人很多時間在一起，你會感到不開心嗎？我們的心裡會不開心，這就是「嫉妒」；看到別的同學得到新的球鞋，心裡又忌妒又羨慕。有嫉妒的感覺是正常的，但之後的行動才是最重要的，看到別人的好，成為我們進步的動力，千萬不要一直陷在忌妒的情緒中，而去傷害別人，傷害別人不能讓你變得更好，只會讓一切變得更糟。我們不能像胡迪（Woody）不小心害到他，因為太嫉妒巴斯光年（Buzz Lightyear），自己也受到傷害。用更寬闊的心欣賞朋友和同學們的優點吧！

Parents

Grandparents

 主題小劇場　MP3 101 ▶

A boy named Andy has a lot of **toy**s that come alive when Andy is not around. On Andy's birthday, all of the toys gather together to find out if any new toys will **replace** them. Just when the toys are relieved to learn that Andy does not get any toys for his birthday, Andy's mother brings out a surprise present. It's a new toy. All of Andy's toys are worried. Woody, Andy's favorite toy, tells everyone not to worry. The toys later meet the new toy. It's Buzz Lightyear, a special space toy. All the toys are surprised by what Buzz Lightyear do, all the toys except Andy starts playing with Buzz Lightyear more often, and takes Buzz Lightyear to bed, where Woody used to be. Woody grows more **jealous.**

One day, Andy is allowed to bring one toy to go out with him. Woody thinks that Andy will very likely **choose** Buzz Lightyear and wants to trap Buzz Lightyear behind Andy's desk. The accident happened and Buzz Lightyear falls out of the window. Suddenly, Andy comes in to take Woody with him to dinner because he cannot see Buzz Lightyear. Woody and Buzz have a fight because of this accident. When they are fighting, they lose Andy and are taken away by another kid. Woody and Buzz Lightyear **save** each other and work together to go back to Andy. When they work together, Woody starts to know Buzz Lightyear more and like him more. In the end, Woody apologize for his misunderstanding and jealousy towards Buzz and they become great friends and share Andy's love.

　　一位名叫安迪（Andy）的小男孩擁有很多的玩具，這些玩具在安迪不在的時候會動起來。安迪生日的那天，所有的玩具都聚在一起，確認安迪是否會得到新玩具來代替他們。正當所有的玩具都放心了，因為安迪沒有拿到新玩具，安迪的媽媽拿出了一個驚喜的禮物，是一個新玩具。安迪的玩具都很擔心，安迪最喜歡的玩具胡迪（Woody）要大家不要擔心。這些玩具不久後見到巴斯光年（Buzz Lightyear），它是個特別的太空玩具，除了胡迪之外，全部的玩具都對巴斯光年的功能感到很驚訝。安迪開始花更多時間跟巴斯光年玩，並帶巴斯光年一起睡覺，這以前是胡迪獨有的，胡迪越來越羨慕巴斯光年。安迪被允許可以帶一個玩具外出，胡迪覺得安迪很可能會帶巴斯光年，想要把巴斯光年困在安迪的桌子後面，沒想到巴斯光年不小心掉出窗外。突然安迪進來，因為看不到巴斯光年，只好帶胡迪出門。因為這個意外，巴斯光年和胡迪打了一架。在兩個人打架的時候，他們和安迪分散了，也被另一個小孩帶走。胡迪和巴斯光年拯救對方，一起合作，重新回到安迪身邊。當他們兩人一起合作時，胡迪更深入認識巴斯光年也更喜歡他。最後胡迪為了自己對巴斯光年的誤會和嫉妒道歉，並一起享受安迪對他們的愛。

 故事單字一起學　MP3 102 ▶

①　toy /tɔɪ/ *n.* 玩具

Please put your toys away

麻煩把你的玩具收起來。

. . . .

②　replace /rɪ`ples/ *v.* 代替

No one can replace you.

沒人可以代替你。

. . . .

③　jealous /ˋdʒɛləs/ *adj.* 嫉妒的

He is jealous of his brother.

他很嫉妒他的哥哥。

. . . .

④　choose /tʃuz/ *v.* 選擇

It's hard to choose between burgers and pizza.

要在漢堡跟披薩之間選一個好難。

. . . .

⑤　save /sev/ *v.* 拯救

They saved me from falling off a cliff.

他們救了我，讓我沒有摔下懸崖。

一句一句練習說　MP3 103 ▶

How do you deal with jealousy?
該怎麼面對嫉妒的感覺？

Communication

❶ Tell this feeling to your parents.
把這種感覺跟你的爸媽說一說。

❷ Work harder.
更努力。

❸ Go mountain climbing and relax.
去爬山然後放鬆。

❹ Focus on what you are good at.
專注在你的強項。

❺ Know yourself is good enough and be confident with yourself.
知道自己已經很好了，對自己有信心。

 主題單字心智圖 MP3 104 ▶

mountain climbing *ph.* 爬山

I go mountain climbing with my parents every week.
我跟我的父母每周都去爬山。

jealousy /ˈdʒɛləsɪ/ *n.* 嫉妒

He hurt his friends because of his jealousy.
他因為嫉妒，傷害了朋友。

deal with *ph.* 處理

He is not good at dealing with stress.
他不擅長排解壓力。

focus /ˈfəʊkəs/ *v.* 專注

I know you're tired, but try to focus.
我知道你很累，
但是試著保持專心。

confident /ˈkɒnfɪd(ə)nt/ *adj.* 自信的

I was starting to feel more confident about the exam.
我開始對自己在這個測驗中的表現有信心了。

Leaving Doesn't Really Mean Forgetting 離開不代表忘記

🎞 帶著寶貝一起讀

　　在電影裡面，安迪（Andy）沒帶胡迪（Woody）去夏令營的時候，胡迪和他的朋友為什麼會擔心呢？翠絲（Jessie）因為主人長大了，她們不再一起玩而感到傷心。當我們轉學或是搬家，我們會因此和身邊的好朋友分離或離開熟悉的環境，但一定要記的分離並不一定代表失去，不要因為害怕失去的悲傷，而拒絕認識新朋友的機會。離開舊的學校，我們會交到新的朋友，認識新的世界，而你們給對方最好的禮物就是共同擁有的回憶。

Parents

Grandparents

 MP3 105 ▶

Andy is going to Cowboy Camp. He wants to bring his toy, Woody. However, he rips Woody's arm by accident and has to **leave** Woody at home. The next day, Andy's mother has a yard sale to **clean out** some things in the house. Woody goes to save one of his toy friends and is stolen by a man named Al. When Woody arrives at Al's house, he finds out there are other cowboy toys. The toys are very excited to see Woody because Woody's coming makes a whole collection of cowboy toys, and they get the chance to be sent to a Japanese museum. However, Woody says he has to go **back** to his owner, Andy.

The toys stop Woody because without Woody, they will have to go back into storage again. One of the toys, Jessie, tells Woody that she used to belong to an owner, Emily. Jessie used to spend lots of time together with Emily. However, Emily grew up and stopped playing with Jessie. Eventually, Emily **gives** Jessie **away**. The cowboy toys tell Woody that owners always grow up and leave their toys behind. Before they are sent to Japan, Woody's toy friends come to save Woody back home. Woody chooses to **stay** with Andy and invite Jessie to go to Andy's house. Woody misses Andy and enjoys playing with him and the other toy friends. Although toys and owners can't walk together to the end, Woody and Andy cherish every step they took together along the way. Now Jessie has a new home, a new owner and a lot of new friends.

　　安迪（Andy）要出發去牛仔夏令營了，他打算帶自己的玩具胡迪（Woody）一起去，可惜他不小心扯破了胡迪的手，只好把胡迪留在家裡。隔天，媽媽為了清掉家裡的一些東西，舉辦了庭院拍賣。胡迪為了救一個玩具朋友，被一個叫艾爾（Al）男人給偷走了。胡迪抵達了艾爾的家，他遇到了其他的牛仔玩具。他們很興奮看到他，因為胡迪的來臨，讓他們成為一個完整的牛仔玩具系列，他們有機會被送到日本的博物館，但是胡迪說他必須要回去找他的主人安迪。

　　這些玩具阻止胡迪，因為少了胡迪，他們又要回去倉庫了。其中一個玩具翠絲（Jessie）告訴胡迪，她以前也有主人，名叫艾蜜莉（Emily），翠絲曾經是艾蜜莉的最愛，她們花很多時間在一起。直到有一天，艾蜜莉長大了，她不再和翠絲玩了，最後，她把翠絲送出去。這些玩具告訴胡迪，所有的主人都會長大，然後留下他們的玩具。發生在翠絲身上的是，也會發生在胡迪身上。艾爾把全部的玩具準備好，要送去日本，包含翠絲和胡迪。在他們被送去日本之前，胡迪的玩具朋友跑來救胡迪和翠絲。胡迪邀請翠絲一起回去安迪的家。胡迪想念安迪也喜歡跟他和其他朋友一起玩。雖然玩具和主人無法一起到永遠，但胡迪和安迪珍惜他們在一起的每一天。現在翠絲有一個新家，一個新主人和許多新朋友。

故事單字一起學　MP3 106 ▶

① **leave** /liv/ *v.* 留下
His shoes left muddy marks on the floor.
他的鞋子在地板上留下泥腳印。

② **clean out** /klin aʊt/ *ph.* 清除
I found these photos while I was cleaning out my closet.
我清理壁櫥時發現這些照片。

③ **back** /bæk/ *adv.* 回原地
It's time for us to go back.
時間到了，我們該回去了。

④ **give away** /gɪv əˋwe/ *ph.* 贈送
She decided to give away her toys.
她決定把她的玩具送出去。

⑤ **stay** /ste/ *v.* 留下
How long are you going to stay in Paris?
你會在巴黎留多久？

一句一句練習說 MP3 107 ▶

How do you make new friends?
怎麼交新朋友？

Communication

❶ You can sign up for language classes.
你可以去上語言課程。

❷ Ask a friend to introduce someone.
請朋友介紹新朋友。

❸ Join a school club.
參加一個學校社團

❹ Look up activities you are interested in.
找你有興趣的活動參加。

❺ Why don't you volunteer?
你可以試著做義工？

主題單字心智圖　MP3 108 ▶

introduce /ɪntrə`djus/ *v.* 介紹

I introduced myself.
我做了自我介紹。

join /dʒɔɪn/ *v.* 參加

Would you like to join us?
你要不要加入我們呢？

place /ples/ *n.* 地方

Do you remember this place?
你還記得這個地方嗎？

activity /æk`tɪvətɪ/ *n.* 活動

There are many activities at the farm every weekend.
農場上每個週末都辦很多活動。

volunteer /vɑlən`tɪr/ *v.* 自願

I volunteered to clean the classroom.
我自願幫忙整理教室。

帶著寶貝一起讀

　　當你設定目標，努力達成，有時當我們達成目標時，發現跟我們想的不一樣，或者有一些變化，必須改變目標，但已經花了好多時間，捨不得放棄，但其實有時候放棄是勇敢的，生命中有太多我們無法掌控的事情了。努力的過程是比結果更重要的。電影中的卡爾本來的目標是保護好他和太太的房子，前往目標的路上經歷許多冒險，房子被破壞了，不得不放棄他的房子，但遇到許多新朋友幫助他。這些冒險讓他了解到放棄原本的目標是沒關係的，因為他和新認識的朋友踏上一趟新的冒險、創造更多美好的回憶。

Parents

Grandparents

主題小劇場　　MP3 109 ▶

Carl, who loves adventures, grows up with Ellie, who shares the same interest with Carl. They love each other very much and get married. When they are both old, Ellie is sent to the hospital. The trip with Ellie never comes true. Carl lives alone after Ellie's death, protecting the house and all their memories. One day, Carl is forced to move their **house**, and Carl decides to use **balloon**s to fly their house to their dream place. A boy, Russell, accidentally flies into the air with Carl. Carl wants to send Russell back, but surprisingly, Russell helps Carl land at a place close to where Carl and Ellie dream to be, near a waterfall.

On the way to the waterfall, they run into a special bird and a talking dog. Carl really wants to get rid of them because they slow him down to the dream place. After the house is set by the waterfall, Carl goes inside the house alone and looks through Ellie's adventure book. He sees what Ellie leaves in the book — 'Thanks for the adventure. Now go have a new one!' and understands that he does not need to **hold on** to Ellie so much. It is okay to **let go of** the house and he needs to save his

friends who are with him in the new adventure. In the end, Carl saves the bird and brings Russell and the dog home with him. Together, they create more **wonderful** memories.

　　喜歡冒險的卡爾（Carl）和艾莉（Ellie）一起長大，艾莉和卡爾有著相同的興趣。他們很相愛，也結了婚。當他們都老了之後，艾利被送進醫院，這趟旅程從沒成真，在這之後，卡爾就自己一個人住，保護著他們的房子以及艾利的回憶。有一天，當卡爾被迫搬出他們的房子時，他決定用氣球，讓房子飛上天，把自己和房子帶到他和艾莉夢想之地。小男孩羅素（Russell）不小心和卡爾一起飛上天了。卡爾想要將羅素送回去，但出乎意料之外的是，羅素幫忙卡爾降落到一個很近卡爾和艾莉夢想中的地方—瀑布旁。

　　在前往瀑布的路上，他們遇到一隻特別的鳥以及一隻會講話的狗，卡爾很想擺脫他們。卡爾真的想要擺脫他們，因為他們拖慢他抵達夢想之地的速度。把房子放到瀑布旁後，卡爾獨自進到房子裡，開始翻艾利的冒險剪貼簿，他看到艾利留在剪貼簿裡的留言後—「謝謝你陪我走過這段旅程，去尋找你的下一段旅程吧！」，他了解到自己不需要如此一直緊抓著艾莉的回憶不放。他應該放棄那個房子，拯救與他一起冒險的新朋友。最後，卡爾救了小鳥並把羅素和小狗帶回家，一起創造更多美好的回憶。

 故事單字一起學　MP3 110 ▶

①　house /haʊs/ *n.* 房子
They live in a lovely house.
他們住在一棟可愛的房子。

- -

②　balloon /bə`lun/ *n.* 氣球
I will bring balloons for his birthday party.
他的生日派對我會帶氣球。

- -

③　hold on /hold ɑn/ *ph.* 緊握
Please hold on to the railing.
請緊握欄杆。

- -

④　let go of /lɛt go ɔv/ *ph.* 放開
Now you can let go of the rope.
現在可以放開繩子了。

- -

⑤　wonderful /`wʌndɚfəl/ *adj.* 極好的
They had a wonderful day.
他們過了非常美好的　天。

一句一句練習說　MP3 111 ▶

**What do I need when I go on
an adventure?**
我去冒險的時候需要什麼？

Communication

❶ I need to bring a water bottle.
我需要帶水瓶。

❷ I will read my map.
我會看地圖。

❸ I can't forget my flashlight.
我不能忘記我的手電筒。

❹ I am going to put everything in my backpack.
我會把全部的東西都放進背包。

❺ I should wear boots.
我應該穿靴子。

 主題單字心智圖　MP3 112 ▶

map /mæp/ *n.* 地圖

Do you know how to read a map?.
你知道怎麼看地圖嗎？

water bottle /ˈwɔtɚ ˈbɑtl/ *n.* 水瓶

Please fill the water bottle with full water.
請幫忙把水瓶裝滿水。

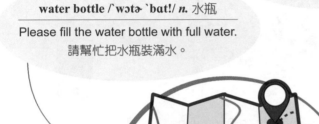

backpack /ˈbækˌpæk/ *n.* 後背包

He puts the books in his backpack.
他把那些書放在他的後背包裡。

boots /buts/ *n.* 靴子

I wear rain boots on a rainy day.
我下雨天穿雨鞋。

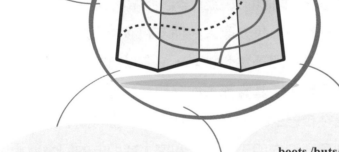

flashlight /ˈflæʃˌlaɪt/ *n.* 手電筒

When you cannot see in the dark, use the flashlight.
在黑暗中看不到的時候，可以使用手電筒。

帶著寶貝一起讀

　　我們要學著去面對失去愛的人的痛，電影裡的辛巴（Simba）失去了他的父親，辛巴非常的傷心，他認為一切都是自己的錯。失去家人、朋友和寵物很難受，失去的感覺很糟，讓人忍不住想逃避，逃避以前的傷心回憶。辛巴最後也了解了，其實死去的父親還是會一直在他的心中，永遠活在自己的記憶裡，陪伴自己。當時間過去，我們還是能夠勇敢迎向明天，想著和家人或朋友的回憶就會得到力量。

Parents

Grandparents

Mufasa the lion is the **king** of the animal kingdom. He and his wife, Sarabi, have a new **son**, Simba. All the animals come to celebrate the birth of the new baby lion and the future king. Mufasa's brother, Scar, is sad and angry that he loses the chance of being the king. Therefore, Scar takes Simba to some dangerous places and tells the curious little lion not to go there again. Simba takes his friend, Nala, to the place and they are attacked. Mufasa saves them in time.

The next day, Scar **trick**s tricks Simba into going to a dangerous rock. Mufasa rushes to save Simba and ends up hanging on a cliff. Instead of saving Mufasa, Scar lets Mufasa fall and kills him. Scar tells Simba it's his fault. Hearing this, Simba runs away, so Scar takes over the country. One day after several years, Simba meets his old friend, Nala, and she tells him to return to the kingdom. Simba is afraid of going back because of the death of his **father**. A baboon tells him although his father is not **around**; he is forever in Simba's heart and support him. Simba's father always to tells him to remember the real self and listen to his own heart. Simba decides to go

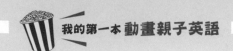
back and take back the kingdom from the evil Scar. Then, Simba realizes the one killing his father is Scar but not himself.

　　獅子木法沙（Mufasa）是動物王國的國王，他和他的太太莎拉碧（Sarabi）剛生了兒子辛巴（Simba），全部的動物都來慶祝新獅子的誕生，他也是未來的國王。木法沙的弟弟刀疤（Scar）對於自己不能當國王感到傷心又生氣。所以，刀疤帶莎拉碧去一些危險的地方，並告訴這隻好奇的小獅子不准再去。辛巴帶了他的朋友娜娜（Nala）去那個地方，結果他們被鬣狗攻擊，好險木法沙及時救了他們。

　　隔天，刀疤把辛巴騙到石頭上，告訴辛巴他的爸爸要給他一個驚喜，刀疤叫鬣狗去嚇一大群動物，讓動物跑過辛巴所在的地方，木法沙衝去救辛巴後，最後掛在懸崖上，而刀疤沒救木法沙，反而讓木法沙掉下去，殺死了他。刀疤告訴辛巴這都是他的錯，聽到這個，辛巴逃走了，而刀疤接管動物王國。幾年過去了，有一天，辛巴遇到他以前的朋友娜娜，娜娜看到辛巴很開心，告訴辛巴他應該回去王國，因為他父親的死，辛巴害怕回家。狒狒先生告訴他雖然他的父親已經不在了，他還是在辛巴的心中支持他。辛巴的父親總是告訴他記得真正的自己，而且傾聽自己的心。辛巴決定回家並從邪惡的刀疤手中奪回王國。他了解到殺死他父親的是刀疤，而不是自己。

 故事單字一起學　MP3 114 ▶

1 **king** /kɪŋ/ *n.* 國王
The king takes good care of his people.
這位國王很照顧他的人民。

2 **son** /sʌn/ *n.* 兒子
He took a picture with his son and daughter.
他和兒子和女兒拍了一張照。

3 **trick** /trɪk/ *v.* 欺騙
They tricked her into telling the truth.
他們騙她說出事實。

4 **father** /ˈfɑðɚ/ *n.* 父親
How old is your father?
你的爸爸幾歲？

5 **around** /əˈraʊnd/ *adv.* 四處
I can't see anyone around.
我四處都沒看到人。

一句一句練習說 MP3 115 ▶

Communication

How do you keep memories?
你如何保存記憶呢？

❶ **You can take more pictures.**
你可以多拍一點照。

❷ **Try to make your own videos.**
試著自己拍影片。

❸ **Write it down as a story in your journal.**
把回憶寫進你的日記本。

❹ **I collect all the photos into an album.**
我把所有照片放在相簿內。

❺ **Keep everything related in a box.**
留下所有相關的東西放在一個箱子內。

主題單字心智圖　MP3 116 ▶

memory /ˈmɛmərɪ/ *n.* 記憶
Jane still has a clear memory of the trip.
珍還很清楚地記得那趟旅行。

journal /ˈdʒɝ-n!/ *n.* 日記
She writes down
everything in her journal.
她把所有事情都記在日記裡。

video /ˈvɪdɪˌo/ *n.* 影片
You can watch videos on the website.
你可以在網站上看影片。

story /ˈstorɪ/ *n.* 故事
I like to listen bedtime stories.
我喜歡聽睡前故事。

collect /kəˈlɛkt/ *v.* 收集
She has collected lots of baseball cards.
她收集了很多棒球卡。

Unit 30 蟲蟲危機 A Bug's Life
Take Up The Responsibility
承擔責任

帶著寶貝一起讀

　　每個人都有自己該負的責任，也就是你應該做的事，例如把自己的作業做好、房間整理好，像準備當皇后的蟻公主雅婷（Atta）的責任就是領導大家，雖然她很緊張，但不管在什麼情況下，她還是把自己的工作做好。而犯錯的時候，也有該負的責任，這表示不找藉口，想辦法解決問題，像電影裡面的飛力（Flik）不小心毀了要給蚱蜢的食物，造成了螞蟻王國的危機，但他沒有逃避，而是負起自己犯錯之後的責任，想了各種解決辦法。想想看自己該負的責任有哪些呢？什麼樣才是負責任呢？

Parents

Grandparents

All the **ant**s are collecting food for some **grasshopper**s. One of the ants is Flik. He wants to invent new things to help other ants to collect. When the food is almost ready and the ants are waiting for the grasshoppers to come, Flik knocks over the food with his invention. The grasshoppers are very angry. The angry grasshoppers tell the ants to prepare the food again and then leave. All the ants are worried. He tries to come up with ideas and suggests that they get help from other **bug**s. Just when no ants think it is possible, Flik volunteers to get help. He sets off alone to find bigger bugs and arrives at the bug city. He meets a group of bugs. Flik thinks the bugs can help him and his fellow ants. He takes the bugs back home with him.

After Flik arrives home, he finds out that the bugs are not as strong as he thinks. Things are now more difficult, but Flik sticks around. To fight off the grasshoppers, Flik plans to make a fake bird because he remembers that grasshoppers are afraid of birds. He leads the bugs and the ants together to finish the bird. They are very close to scaring away all the grasshoppers. When 'the bird plan' fails, the grasshoppers are angry and demand to know who came up up with the idea. Flik tells the grasshoppers that it is him and he is hit badly. However, Flik is not scared. He stands up for himself and the other ants. The ants finally scare away the grasshoppers. Flik always **owns up** to his mistakes and tries to solve problems. The ants get rid of the the threatening grasshoppers and live peacefully.

　　所有的螞蟻都在為蚱蜢收集食物，其中一隻是飛力（Flik），他喜歡發明新東西。當食物準備的差不多時，所有的螞蟻都去等蚱蜢的到來，但飛力的發明卻不小心把食物給弄倒了，蚱蜢十分的生氣。生氣的蚱蜢要螞蟻再重新準備的食物，然後就離開了。全部的螞蟻都很擔心。他試著想出新主意，並建議他們找其他昆蟲來幫忙。螞蟻們覺得這是不可能的，飛力自願去尋求支援。飛力獨自出發去找更大的昆蟲，並來到昆蟲城市。他遇到一群昆蟲，飛力認為這些昆蟲可以幫助自己和螞蟻同胞，就帶著這些蟲一起回家去。

　　飛力到家後，發現原來這些蟲不像他想像的那樣強大。現在事情更棘手了，但飛力繼續堅持。飛力想起蚱蜢怕鳥，於是計畫造一隻假鳥，來打敗蚱蜢。他帶領那些昆蟲和螞蟻，他們合力完成了假鳥。他們差一點就要把全部的蚱蜢嚇跑。當假鳥計畫失敗後，蚱蜢很生氣，並要求知道是誰想出來的主意。飛力告訴蚱蜢是他，於是被打得很慘。但是，飛力完全不怕，他為了自己和其他螞蟻挺身而出。螞蟻們最終趕走蚱蜢。因為飛力總是勇於承認自己的錯誤，並嘗試解決問題，螞蟻們才得以擺脫蚱蜢的威脅，過著平和的日子。

故事單字一起學　MP3 118 ▶

1 **ant** /ænt/ *n.* 螞蟻
You see many ants in the summer.
夏天會看到很多螞蟻。

2 **grasshopper** /ˋgræsˌhɑpɚ/ *n.* 蚱蜢
How high can a grasshopper jump?
蚱蜢可以跳多高呢？

3 **admit** /ədˋmɪt/ *v.* 承認
Why don't you just admit that you took it?
你為什麼不乾脆承認是你拿的？

4 **bug** /bʌg/ *n.* 蟲子
I don't like bugs.
我不喜歡蟲蟲。

5 **own up** /on ʌp/ *ph.* 承認犯錯
It's important to own up to your mistakes.
承認自己的錯誤是很重要的。

一句一句練習說 MP3 119 ▶

What do you say when you feel sorry?
當你覺得很抱歉時，你會說什麼？

Communication

❶ I am sorry I said hurtful words.
我很抱歉說了傷人的話。

❷ It was wrong to take your toys.
拿你的玩具是錯的。

❸ It was my fault.
這都是我的錯。

❹ I did not mean it.
我不是有意的。

❺ It will not happen again.
這不會再發生了。

 主題單字心智圖 MP3 120 ▶

wrong /rɔŋ/ *adj.* 錯誤的

She admitted that she was wrong.
她承認她錯了。

hurtful /ˈhɝtfəl/ *adj.* 傷害的

What he said was hurtful.
他說的話很傷人。

fault /fɔlt/ *n.* 錯誤

It's my fault your doll is broken.
你的娃娃壞掉都是我的錯。

happen /ˈhæpən/ *v.* 發生

When did the car accident happen?
車禍是什麼時候發生的？

mean /min/ *v.* 意思

What does "spectacular" mean?
"spectacular" 是指什麼意思？

Bigger And Stronger Than You Think
你比想像中更強大

帶著寶貝一起讀

在你的學校有身材比較瘦小的同學嗎？在學校的時候，當我們長的不是特別高壯，或是個性比較安靜時，別人可能會以為我們很弱小，因此欺負我們或嘲笑我們。當你因為自己的外表或是個性受到欺負的時候，不要因此感到自卑，勇敢為自己發聲。因為我們比自己或別人想像的還要強大，只要相信自己，給自己一點時間，多多與自己相處，看見並發揮自己的優點，讓自己和別人看到最棒的自己。

Parents　　　**Grandparents**

Arlo is a lot smaller than other **dinosaur**s. He cannot do many things his sister and brothers do because he is **weak**er and he is afraid of many things. His brother always makes fun of him. Nevertheless, his parents still love him very much and think he will become stronger someday. One day, Arlo's father tells Arlo to catch the beast that steals their food with a trap. Arlo sets up the trap and catches the beast. It is a **wild** human boy. Arlo is scared by the boy and screams. The boy runs away. Arlo's father brings Arlo with him to look for the boy. It starts to rain. The lightning and thunder scare Arlo again. Just then, the river starts to overflow. Arlo's father puts Arlo in a safe place before he gets washed away by the **flood**.

After Arlo's father is gone, the rest of the family works hard to stay alive. One day, Arlo finds the human boy eating their food again. He chases the boy into the wild. The boy finds some food for Arlo and they get to spend time together. Arlo takes the boy with him and together they begin a trip back to Arlo's home. On their way back, Arlo learns from other dinosaurs. A dinosaur tells Arlo that everyone has fear. There is no way you can run away from your own fear, but you can get through your fear. Arlo gradually becomes braver. He frees himself from tangled plants, saves the boy from drowning and protects him against the other dinosaurs. In the end, Arlo leaves the boy with the boy's new family and walks back home alone.

　　阿羅（Arlo）比其他恐龍還小很多，很多事情他都沒辦法像自己的哥哥或姊姊做得那麼好，因為他比較虛弱，也害怕很多東西。但是他的父母還是很愛他，覺得他總有一天會變得很堅強。有一天，阿羅的爸爸告訴阿羅用陷阱去抓一隻都偷吃他們的食物的野獸。阿羅設下了陷阱，並抓到了野獸，那是一個野生的小男孩。阿羅被小男孩嚇到，還尖叫，男孩逃跑之後，阿羅的爸爸因為阿羅放走了男孩而對他大叫。阿羅的爸爸帶著阿羅去找回小男孩，但突然開始下起雨，阿羅又被閃電和打雷嚇到，就在這時候，河水開始上漲，阿羅的爸爸把阿羅放到安全的地方，然後就被洪水沖走了。

　　阿羅的父親離開之後，剩下的家人努力活下來。有一天，阿羅發現那個男孩又來偷吃他們的東西，阿羅跑去追他，來到荒野。男孩找了一些食物給阿羅吃，他們相處了一段時間，阿羅帶著男孩一起出發回阿羅家。在回家的路上，阿羅和其他恐龍學了很多，其中一隻恐龍告訴阿羅，大家都有害怕的事情，你沒辦法逃離你自己的恐懼，但你可以克服你的恐懼。阿羅慢慢變得更勇敢，他能讓自己脫離植物的綑綁，從水中救出小男孩，或被其他恐龍攻擊。最後阿羅把小男孩留給他的新家人，自己走回家。

 故事單字一起學　MP3 122 ▶

❶ dinosaur /ˋdaɪnəˌsɔr/ *n.* 恐龍
The T-Rex is his favorite dinosaur.
暴龍是他最愛的恐龍。

❷ weak /wik/ *adj.* 虛弱的
My grandmother is now too weak to move.
我的外婆現在太虛弱，動不了。

❸ wild /waɪld/ *adj.* 野生的
Please be careful of wild animals.
請小心野生動物。

❹ flood /flʌd/ *n.* 洪水
The flood destroyed the streets.
洪水摧毀了街道。

❺ attack /əˋtæk/ *v.* 攻擊
The bear attacked a man.
那隻熊攻擊了一個人。

一句一句練習說 MP3 123 ▶

How can you help when you see bullying?
你看到霸凌可以怎麼幫忙？

Communication

❶ Do not join in.
千萬不要加入。

❷ Always tell an adult and the teacher.
一定要告訴大人和老師。

❸ Try your best to protect yourself.
努力保護好自己。

❹ You can stand up to the bully when it's safe.
安全的時候可以抵抗霸凌者。

❺ Do not stay silent.
不要保持沉默。

主題單字心智圖　MP3 124 ▶

bully /ˋbʊlɪ/ v. 霸凌

Don't join the bully and always tell adults.
千萬不要加入霸凌和記得告訴大人。

adult /əˋdʌlt/ n. 成人

Sarah can't wait to become an adult.
莎拉等不及要變大人了。

protect /prəˋtɛkt/ v. 保護

I'll protect you from bad people.
我會保護你，讓壞人不要接近你。

safe /sef/ adj. 安全的

It's not safe to go out so late.
那麼晚出去不安全。

stand up to /stænd ʌp tu/ ph. 勇於抵抗

We should stand up to bullies.
我們都應該反霸凌。

Unit 32 瓦力 WALL-E
Feel Alive Again
感受生命的活力

帶著寶貝一起讀

　　你有手機嗎？隨著科技越來越進步，我們能更快速和便利與人溝通，用手機或平板隨時都可以打電話或傳訊息，但我們也少了一些和人面對面講話的機會，就像「瓦力」中的人類，享受方便的科技，節省時間，卻少了許多生命中的真實感動，例如：坐在身旁的人透過畫面聊天，人與人之間好久沒有觸碰到對方了。其實好好善用科技，不要過度依賴和沉迷，取得一個平衡，好好享受科技的便利。可以和小朋友規範使用手機的時間，不要過度使用科技產品，而忘記與人真實的接觸！

Parents

Grandparents

On the deserted **Earth**, one of the cleaning robots, WALL-E, cleans up the garbage left on Earth every day. One day, a robot, EVE, is sent to the Earth to look for living plants. WALL-E is attracted to EVE right away and wants to hold her **hand**. In order to do that, WALL-E shows EVE the plant which is Eve looking for, so this sends EVE back to her mother ship soon. WALL-E secretly gets on the ship as well. They go back to the spaceship Axiom, where human beings **live** now. Humans have been living inside Axiom for hundreds of years. Life is very convenient here. People only sit on floating chairs that move on their own and enjoy everything that is prepared by machines. People do not look at anything but their screens and only talk to each other through computers. They have never **touch**ed each other.

When WALL-E gets into the spaceship, he wants to find EVE. There he sees human beings for the first time. Later, WALL-E meets another woman and helps her see the things around her. This man and woman accidentally touch each other's hand, for the first time to **feel** another human being.

When the computer in Axiom does not let the people go back to the Earth, WALL-E, EVE, and some people and robots work together to send everyone back to the Earth. People can finally talk to each other face to face and together help the Earth flourish again.

在被遺棄的地球上，其中一隻清理用機器人瓦力（WALL-E）每天都在清除留在地球上的垃圾。有一天，另一隻機器人伊芙（EVE）被送到地球上來找植物。瓦力馬上被伊芙給吸引，而且想握她的手，為了能接近伊芙，瓦力帶她去看植物，植物正是伊芙在找的，這反而讓伊芙很快地回到母艦，瓦力也偷偷上船。他們回到了現在人類著的太空船公理號（Axiom）。人類已經在公理號住了數百年了。在這裡生活非常的方便。人們只要坐在會自己移動的漂浮椅子，並享受為他們準備好的所有東西。人們除了螢幕之外，什麼都不看，而與人溝通也只透過電腦，他們從沒碰過對方。

等瓦力到達太空船裡時，他開始找伊芙，他第一次看到人類，後來瓦力也遇到另一個女人，並幫助她看到周邊的事物。這個男人和女人不小心碰到對方的手，而這是第一次他們感受到另一個人類。當公理號上的電腦不讓人類回到地球時，瓦力、伊芙、一些人類和機器人一起合作，讓大家能順利回到地球。人們終於看著對方的臉說話，而且大家一起幫助地球再次繁榮。

 故事單字一起學　MP3 126 ▶

❶ **Earth** /ɝθ/ *n.* 地球
We should protect the Earth.
我們應該保護地球。

. . . .

❷ **hand** /hænd/ *n.* 手
We shake hands to greet each other.
我們握手來打招呼。

. . . .

❸ **live** /lɪv/ *v.* 住
I live in San Francisco now.
我現在住在舊金山。

. . . .

❹ **touch** /tʌtʃ/ *v.* 觸碰
Please do not touch the painting.
請不要碰這幅畫。

. . . .

❺ **feel** /fil/ *v.* 感受
The sheet feels so soft.
這床單摸起來好軟。

我的第一本動畫親子英語

一句一句練習說 MP3 127 ▶

What do you do in your free time?
你們在休閒的時候做什麼活動？

Communication

① Go to a different restaurant together every week.
每個禮拜一起去一間不同的餐廳。

② Surf on the Internet and play online games.
上網和玩線上遊戲。

③ Play basketball or go to swim.
打籃球和游泳。

④ Chat with my parents and friends.
和我的父母和朋友聊聊天。

⑤ Go outdoors to play and picnic on the weekend.
周末時去戶外玩耍和野餐。

主題單字心智圖　MP3 128 ▶

free time 空閒的時候，休閒時間

Mostly I do sports with
my friends in my free time.
通常休閒的時候，我會和朋友一起運動。

outdoor /ˌaʊtˈdɔ:(r)/ *adj.* 戶外的

Riding the bike is the most
popular outdoor activities in Taiwan.
騎腳踏是在台灣最受歡迎的
戶外運動。

trip /trɪp/ *n.* 旅行

She takes a trip abroad every year.
她每年都出國旅行。

chat /tʃæt/ *v.* 聊天

She laughed and chatted
happily with the other women.
她開心的笑著和另一位
女士聊天。

surf / sə:f/ *v.* 瀏覽
（指在電腦網路上、或在有趣的電視節目上隨意地搜索資料）

My grandmother now learns to surf on the Internet.
我的祖母現在學著上網。

Unit 33 花木蘭Mulan

Push the Boundaries
突破限制

帶著寶貝一起讀

　　你覺得男生應該是什麼樣子？女生又應該是什麼樣子呢？我們都覺得男生好像比較勇敢，女生應該要文靜；男生應該穿藍色，當醫生或警察，女生要穿粉紅色，當護士或老師。不過有時候我們喜歡的事情可能跟其他人不一樣，不過也不用擔心，勇敢做自己，雖然可能會很辛苦，但對自己誠實，然後勇敢的、努力的追求自己的夢想。相信最後會得到很大的快樂喔！希望我們都能就像花木蘭一樣，不管男生或女生，都可以當一個勇敢的人，不要被性別所限制了自己的任何機會唷！

Parents

Grandparents

Fa Mulan is the daughter of a farmer in China. The story begins when Fa Mulan is in matchmaker's house, waiting to be set up with a **husband** soon because a good girl should marry early to honor her family. However, she embarrassed herself there and her family as well because she is different from other girls. A few days later, some men arrive at Mulan's village to get a **man** from each family to join the **army**. Mulan's father is chosen because he is the only man in the family. Mulan is sad because she knew well that her father is too old and weak to join the army. She stands up to speak up but is told not to speak when men are talking. Therefore, she steals her father's sword and horse and cuts her hair. She dresses up as a man and goes into army instead of her dad.

Mulan arrives at the training camp with her horse and meets one of her family dragons, Mushu, who says he comes to protect her. At the camp, Mulan tries to act like a man to pass the hard training. Although she is a girl, she is not afraid of hard training and never gives up. She tries her best to catch up or better than other men and impress the Captain, Li Shang.

Her **wisdom** saves a lot of people in a fight. However, Mulan gets hurt and after a checkup, everyone finds out she is a **woman**, so leave her behind and continue their journey. In the end, Mulan saves everybody's life from their enemy, Shang Yu again and receives gifts from the emperor and falls in love with the Captain.

　　花木蘭（Fa Mulan）是個中國農夫的女兒故事從木蘭在媒人的屋子裡等待快一點被許配給一個男人，因為一個好女孩應該早日結婚以光宗耀祖。然而她在那裡丟了自己和家人的臉，因為她和其他女孩不太一樣。幾天後，一些男人來花木蘭的村子，從每個家庭中徵求一個男人從軍，因為是家裡唯一的男人，木蘭的父親被選中了。木蘭很傷心，因為她清楚知道，她父親太老又虛弱，不能從軍。她站出來為父親說話，但被制止了，因為男人們正在說話。於是她偷走父親的劍和馬、剪了自己的頭髮，打扮成男人後代替自己的父親出發了。木蘭和她的馬來到訓練營並遇到了家族的龍—木須（Mushu），他說他是來保護木蘭的。在訓練營裡，木蘭試著表現得像個男人好通過嚴格的訓練。雖然她是一個女生，她不害怕辛苦的訓練也不因此退縮。 她盡全力跟上其他人，甚至比其他男人都厲害，將軍李翔都對她刮目相看。木蘭的智慧在一場仗役中救了不少人，然而，木蘭受了傷，在檢查之後，大家都知道她是個女人，所以將她留下並繼續他們的旅程。最後，木蘭再次從敵人單于手中拯救大家，收到了皇帝的禮物並與將軍陷入愛河。

MP3 130 ▶

❶ husband /ˋhʌzbənd/ *n.* 先生
She is going to Italy with her husband.
她要和她老公去義大利。

❷ man /mæn/ *n.* 男人
She is talking to the man.
她在跟那個男人講話。

❸ army /ˋɑrmɪ/ *n.* 軍隊
I'm going to join the army.
我要去當兵了。

❹ wisdom /ˋwɪzdəm/ *n.* 智慧
She is a woman of great wisdom.
她是位很有智慧的女人。

❺ woman /ˋwʊmən/ *n.* 女人
She is a brave woman.
她是位很勇敢的女人。

一句一句練習說 MP3 131 ▶

What can girls and boys do?
女孩和男孩可以做什麼？

Communication

❶ Boys can wear pink clothes.
男孩子可以穿粉紅色衣服。

❷ Girls can have short hair.
女孩子可以留短頭髮。

❸ Men can be nurses.
男人可以當護士。

❹ Women can be doctorrs.
女人可以當醫生。

❺ The most important thing is to be real you.
最重要的是做自己。

 MP3 132 ▶

wear /wɛr/ *v.* 穿

What are you going to wear to the party?
你要穿什麼去派對？

gender /ˈdʒɛndɚg/ *n.* 性別

We talked about some gender issues.
我們聊了一些性別議題。

short /ʃɔrt/ *adj.* 短的

She's shorter than her brother.
她比弟弟還要矮。

nurse /ˈnɚ:s/ *n.* 護士

He is one of male nurses in the hospital.
他是許多醫院男護士中的其中一位。

astronaut /ˈæstrəˌnɔt/ *n.* 太空人

She wants to be an astronaut when she grows up.
她長大想當太空人。

帶著寶貝一起讀

　　生活中我們一定會遇到一些問題，當我們遇到問題時，一開始都會覺得很挫折，有時候甚至不敢告訴別人，想要靠自己的力量解決。就像「歡樂好聲音」的無尾熊巴斯特（Buster）發現劇場即將面臨倒閉，他決定舉辦一場歌唱比賽，這是一個很棒的方法，但是他欺騙大家有一大筆獎金，他的謊話製造出更多的問題。最後當他誠實面對問題，大家還是樂意幫助他，果然在眾人的幫助下，他們成功重建劇場。遇到問題時，應該選擇勇敢面對，絕對不要說謊或試圖掩蓋問題，如果你不正視問題，就不能真正解決問題。

Parents

Grandparents

主題小劇場　　MP3 133 ▶

Buster, the koala bear is the owner of a **theater**. Sadly, the **future** of the theater does not look very bright. Buster decides to hold a singing **competition**. The winner of the competition can get a large prize, so a lot of animals show up for the competition. When these animals start practicing for the show, there are gradually more problems in the theater. It lacks electricity and there is a hole on the roof. Buster also owes money to the bank. Worst of all, a flood completely destroys the theater and then all the animals find out that there is actually no **prize**. They leave with anger because they think they are fooled.

Buster is very depressed. He loses his theater to the bank and can only wash cars to make money. However, when he hears the elephant, Meena, sing beautifully, he decides to give it try again. The selected animal and Buster build a **stage**. That night, all the animals perform on the stage. Some of them dance; some of them play the piano, and some of them sing. The show goes perfectly and everyone loves it. Now Buster does not have to worry. Not only does he win a group of new

friends, he also gets enough money to buy the theater and rebuild it.

　　無尾熊巴斯特（Buster）是劇場的老闆，可惜的是劇場的未來看起來並不光明。為了讓生意好轉，巴斯特覺得舉辦一場歌唱比賽應該會是個好方法，他為了這場比賽印了很多傳單，傳單上寫著如果贏得比賽，就可以得到一大筆獎金，這些傳單意外的被吹到鎮上四處。隔天，一大堆動物跑來參加比賽，巴斯特選了一些動物繼續留下來比賽。這些動物開始為了表演練習，同時劇場的問題越來越多，劇場沒電了，屋頂上還有洞，而且巴斯特還欠銀行錢，最慘的是，一場水災摧毀了劇場，然後所有的動物發現其實並沒有比賽獎金。他們很生氣地離去因為覺得自己被欺騙了。

　　巴斯特感到非常沮喪，他的劇場被銀行給收去，只好靠洗車來賺錢。好險巴斯特聽到大象米娜（Meena）自己在唱歌，唱得非常美。巴斯特想出一個新點子，他將全部的動物都找來，他們自己建了一個舞台。那天晚上，所有的動物都上台表演，有人跳舞，有人彈琴，有人唱歌。這場表演進行的非常順利，所有的人都很喜歡。現在巴斯特不用擔心了，他不只得到了一群新朋友，他還因此得到足夠的錢買回並重建劇場。

 故事單字一起學 MP3 134 ▶

1 **theater** /ˋθɪətɚ/ *n.* 劇場
Let's watch a musical in a theater.
我們一起去劇場看一齣音樂劇吧。

2 **future** /ˋfjutʃɚ/ *n.* 未來
I want to be a pilot in the future.
未來我想當機長。

3 **competition** /ˌkɑmpəˋtɪʃən/ *n.* 比賽
She entered the dance competition.
她參加了跳舞比賽。

4 **prize** /praɪz/ *n.* 獎賞
They won the first prize.
他們贏得第一名。

5 **stage** /stedʒ/ *n.* 舞台
Standing on the stage makes me nervous.
站在舞台上讓我覺得很緊張。

一句一句練習說　MP3 135 ▶

Communication

What makes you happy?
什麼會讓你開心？

❶ I can go to a concert with my friends.
我可以和朋友一起去演唱會。

❷ I can have the pocket money.
我有零用錢。

❸ I get an A on my reading test.
我在閱讀測驗中得到一個A。

❹ I have time to exercise every day.
我每天都有時間運動。

❺ I travel to Europe with my family.
我跟家人到歐洲旅行。

 主題單字心智圖　MP3 136 ▶

concert /ˈkɒnsə(r)t/ *n.* 演唱會

I am going to a concert next month.
下個月我要去參加一個演唱會。

reading /ˈriːdɪŋ/ *n.* 閱讀能力

My brother is having difficulties with his reading.
我的兒子閱讀時有點吃力。

exercise /ˈɛksəˌsaɪz/ *v.* 運動

Walking is great exercise.
走路是個很好的運動。

Europe /ˈjʊərəp/ *n.* 歐洲

I would like to visit Europe most.
我最希望去歐洲旅遊。

pocket money /ˈpɒk.ɪt ˌmʌn.i/ n. 零用錢

How much pocket money do you get?
你得到多少零用錢？

帶著寶貝一起讀

　　你羨慕某些人的生活或是他能做到的事嗎？當我們看到別人穿很漂亮的衣服和去度假，羨慕不已，再看看自己，覺得自己的生活好無趣。雖然這樣讓我們有動力要更努力，不過每個人都有不同的辛苦，也都有自己的優點，就像電影裡的雷夫，他常羨慕別人，也想得到別人擁有的，但是他沒想到自己身為遊戲裡的一個反派角色，卻是遊戲裡不可或缺的一員，他以為沒用的「破壞」專長也能在緊急時刻發揮功用。比起羨慕別人、懷疑自己，更重要的是認識並接受真正的自己、去做自己享受的事，並得到內心真正的快樂。

Parents

Grandparents

 MP3 137 ▶

"Wreck-It Ralph" is a character in a video game. Every day, when all the game characters are off work, he will go back to the dump he lives on and **envy** the good guy in the game, "Fix-It Felix", and the **medal**s he can win. Felix is popular because he helps people fix things. On the other hand, all Ralph does is break things. Everyone is cheering for Felix and tells Ralph that he is just a bad guy that **wreck**s things. This upsets Ralph. He destroys everything and leaves. He decides to go out and win his own medal. He will show everyone that he can be a **hero**, too.

Ralph hears that he can get a medal from other games and ends up in a game called 'Sugar Rush'. Meanwhile, Ralph's game is shut down because he is missing. Felix goes to find Ralph. However, after Felix enters 'Sugar Rush' to bring Ralph back, he is kept in a room by the evil character. Everything he touches becomes stronger, and everything is hard for him. Ralph saves Felix from the room by breaking the door. He also fights with the evil character to save Felix. In the end, medals are no longer important to Ralph and he finally **accept**s who he is. He realizes that although he is a bad guy in his game, there is no one he would rather be than himself. Ralph returns to his own game and the game is finally working again. Now Ralph likes his life and enjoys being Wreck-It Ralph. Everyone likes Wreck-It Ralph.

破壞王雷夫（Wreck-It Ralph）是個遊戲裡的角色。每天等所有的角色都下班時，他就會回到他住的垃圾場，然後羨慕遊戲裡的好人角色阿修（Fix-It Felix），以及他可以得到的獎牌。阿修很受歡迎，因為他會幫忙大家修理東西，反之雷夫只會破壞東西。每一個都喜歡阿修，大家都為阿修歡呼並告訴雷夫，他只是一個破壞東西的壞傢伙。這讓雷夫十分生氣，他把摧毀所有的東西然後就離開了，他決定要出去自己贏獎牌，他會讓大家看到，他也可以當個英雄。

雷夫聽說他可以從其他遊戲贏得獎牌，最終來到一個叫做「糖果賽車」（Sugar Rush）的遊戲。同時，因為雷夫的消失，他的遊戲被關掉了，阿修必須找到雷夫，然而，阿修為了帶回雷夫，進到「糖果賽車」之後，卻被那邪惡的角色關進一個房間。因為他碰到的東西只會變得更堅固，每一件事對他來說都很難。雷夫打破門，把阿修救了出來，他也和那邪惡的角色打了一架。最終，獎牌對雷夫再也不重要，他也接受了他自己，他了解到雖然他是遊戲裡的反派角色，但他也不想成為別人。雷夫回到自己的遊戲，遊戲終於又可以正常運作了。現在的雷夫喜歡自己的生活，也享受自己破壞王雷夫的身份。

 MP3 138 ▶

❶ **envy** /ˈɛnvɪ/ *v.* 羨慕
Sometimes I envy my friends.
有時候我會羨慕我的朋友。

⋯⋯⋯⋯⋯⋯⋯⋯⋯⋯⋯⋯⋯⋯⋯⋯⋯⋯

❷ **medal** /ˈmɛdl̩/ *n.* 獎牌
He won a medal for the country.
他為國家贏得了一面獎牌。

⋯⋯⋯⋯⋯⋯⋯⋯⋯⋯⋯⋯⋯⋯⋯⋯⋯⋯

❸ **wreck** /rɛk/ *v.* 破壞
I have wrecked my only chance.
我破壞了我唯一的機會。

⋯⋯⋯⋯⋯⋯⋯⋯⋯⋯⋯⋯⋯⋯⋯⋯⋯⋯

❹ **hero** /ˈhɪro/ *n.* 英雄
He's the hero of our country.
他是我們國家的英雄。

⋯⋯⋯⋯⋯⋯⋯⋯⋯⋯⋯⋯⋯⋯⋯⋯⋯⋯

❺ **accept** /əkˈsept/ *v.* 接受
They accepted the boy with open arms.
他們十分熱情地接受了那個男孩。

一句一句練習說 MP3 139 ▶

How can I make my life more interesting?

我如何讓我的生活更有趣？

Communication

❶ You can learn new things like riding a bike.
你可以學習新的事物，像是騎腳踏車。

❷ You can find a hobby.
你可以找到一種嗜好。

❸ I read comic books and stories.
我會看漫畫和讀故事。

❹ You can plant some flowers in the garden.
你可以在花園種種植物。

❺ I will help other people.
我要去幫助其他人。

 主題單字心智圖　MP3 140 ▶

bike /baɪk/ *n.* 腳踏車

I love riding a bike in the park.
我熱愛在公園騎腳踏車。

interesting /ˈɪntərɪstɪŋ/ *adj.* 有趣的

It is interesting to hear his stories.
聽他的故事很有趣

hobby /ˈhɑbɪ/ *n.* 嗜好

Jennifer's hobby is collecting stamps.
珍妮佛的嗜好是收集郵票。

garden /ˈgɑrdn/ *n.* 花園

She takes a walk in the garden every afternoon.
她每個下午都在花園散步。

comic book /ˈkɑmɪk bʊk/ *n.* 漫畫書

He enjoys reading comic books.
他很喜歡看漫畫書。

Unit 36 海洋奇緣 Moana

Just Fix It
改過來就好！

帶著寶貝一起讀

面對錯誤你會有什麼感覺呢？ 你都怎麼做呢？

犯了錯千萬不要太過自責，其實學習面對犯錯是很重要的。發生錯誤時可以想想是如何發生的，然後該如何解決，趁機訓練自己解決問題的技巧，也能讓自己越來越堅強，遇到更大的困難的時候就不會被打敗。錯誤不是失敗，錯誤幫助你修正，讓你更接近成功。而且有時候錯誤，也可能是出乎意料之外的成功喔。所以勇敢地擁抱錯誤吧！

Parents

Grandparents

主題小劇場　MP3 141 ▶

On an island, a legend is being told. A demigod, Maui, stole a goddess, Te Fiti's heart, and this makes the goddess very angry. She turned into a monster and cursed the world. On the island lives the chief's daughter, Moana. One day, Moana's grandmother tells her that she is chosen to find Maui to return the heart of Te Fiti. Moana sets on her journey and with the help from the ocean, she finds Maui. She finally convinces Maui to go with her and return the heart to stop the disasters from happening again to her people.

The two sail out into the ocean on Moana's boat. Before they can return the heart, they must find Maui's hook, which makes Maui powerful. With the hook, they continue their journey. They are finally close to where they can return the heart, where they are stopped by the monster. Maui tries to fight the monster but fails. Maui wants to quit but Moana even tries to move the boat forward. Maui's hook is broken and he becomes so angry that leaves Moana alone on the boat. Moana is sad and doesn't want to continue. Fortunately, Moana meets her grandma's spirit which reminds her of who she is. She decides to return the heart by herself. Maui rushes back to help Moana. Together, they return the heart and the monster turns into Te Fiti. Maui **apologize**s to Te Fiti and is forgiven. Both Moana and Maui **overcome** their mistakes and complete their missions successfully. After the journey and the mistakes they have fixed, they have grown into better selves. The world is saved as well.

在一個小島上，有個傳說正在被講述，半神半人毛伊（Maui）偷了女神塔菲提（Te Fiti）的海洋之心，這讓女神非常生氣，她變身為一個怪物，詛咒了世界。 而這個島上住著酋長的女兒莫娜（Moana），有一天，莫娜的奶奶告訴莫娜，她被選上要找到毛伊，並帶他去歸還海洋之心。莫娜出發了，並在海洋的幫助之下，找到了毛伊。她總算說服毛伊要跟她一起去歸還海洋之心。兩人搭著莫娜的船出發了，在歸還海洋之心以前，他們必須找到能讓毛伊強壯的魚鉤，有了魚鉤之後，他們繼續前進，終於來到了歸還海洋之心的地方，但他們被怪物阻擋。毛伊試著打敗怪物但失敗了，毛伊想要停下來但莫娜卻繼續讓船往前。毛伊的魚鉤因此壞掉了，毛伊變得非常憤怒，留下莫娜一人。莫娜十分傷心，也不想再繼續了，幸好在此時莫娜看見奶奶的靈魂，奶奶提醒她記得自己是誰。莫娜決定獨自去歸還海洋之心，毛伊趕回來幫忙。兩人一起還回海洋之心，而怪物因此變回女神塔菲提，毛伊向塔菲提道歉，並得到原諒。莫娜和毛伊都克服了自己的錯誤，並成功完成任務，經過這趟旅程和修正自己的錯誤後，他們都成長了、變得更好，而世界也得到拯救。

 故事單字一起學　MP3 142 ▶

①　island /ˋaɪlənd/ *n.* 島
Taiwan is an island.
台灣是座島嶼。

②　heart /hɑrt/ *n.* 心、心臟
Follow your heart.
跟隨你的心。

③　ocean /ˋoʃən/ *n.* 海洋
The Pacific Ocean is the biggest ocean.
太平洋是最大的海洋。

④　apologize /əˋpɑləˏdʒaɪz/ *v.* 道歉
You need to apologize to your brother.
你要跟你弟弟道歉。

⑤　overcome /ovɚˋkʌm/ *v.* 克服
She must overcome the difficulties.
她必須要克服困難。

一句一句練習說 MP3 143 ▶

@#$%^

What do you do when you make a mistake?

犯錯了可以怎麼做？

Communication

❶ I can fix my mistake.

我可以修正我的錯誤。

❷ I can ask parents and teachers for help.

我可以請父母和老師幫我。

❸ I will remember this experience and not make same mistake again.

我會記住這次的經驗，下次不要再犯錯。

❹ I will say I'm sorry.

我可以說我很抱歉。

❺ I will bravely to face my mistakes.

我會勇敢面對錯誤。

 主題單字心智圖　MP3 144 ▶

mistake /mɪˋstek/ *n.* 錯誤

I can learn from my mistakes.
我可以從我的錯誤學到很多。

fix /fɪks/ *v.* 修理

He is going to fix my car.
他要幫我修理車子。

help /hɛlp/ *v.* 幫忙

Do you need some help with your homework?
你需要人幫忙你做作業嗎？

brave /brev/ *adj.* 勇敢的

She is a brave girl.
她是位很有勇氣的女孩。

think /θɪŋk/ *v.* 想

I'll think about it.
讓我想一下。

在家就能輕鬆打造親子英語教室
小學生必備的基礎學科通通有

將家庭教育、英語學習和學校課程巧妙融入本書，內容涵蓋天文、地理、生物、科學、人文藝術，主題引導學習，讓小朋友聽得懂，讀得下去。是兼具實用和趣味的親子英語共讀書。

我的第一本萬用親子英語 (附MP3)
定價 NT$ 399
ISBN：9789869528894
書系編號：文法/生活英語系列 006
書籍規格：224頁/18K/普通級/全彩印刷/平裝附光碟

結合自然發音與KK音標的圖解發音書
解決學習發音的困擾

單元特色：
◎50個音標+6組字尾聯音：迅速辨認音標與發音規則
◎8組繞口令：透過反覆練習繞口令，矯正英文發音，加強口齒伶俐度
◎老師獨門音節劃分法：劃分音節，輕鬆讀出英文長字

圖解英文發音二重奏：自然發音、KK音標 (附MP3)
定價 NT$ 369
ISBN：9789869191586
書系編號：Learn Smart 055
書籍規格：288頁/18K/普通級/雙色印刷/平裝附光碟

運用思考力、創意力和英語力
編織屬於自己的童話故事

加入許多科技元素、高科技產品於故事情節中，融入許多道地語彙及美式幽默，更將童話故事中人物善惡對調，kuso的情節激起許多風波和笑點，引領讀者品味不同的故事。學習另一種活潑、新穎的說法，讓你的口語英文更自然。

童話奇緣：Follow Kuso英語童話，來一場穿越時空之旅 (附MP3)
定價 NT$ 380
ISBN：9789869191555
書系編號：Learn Smart 052
書籍規格：332頁/18K/普通級/雙色印刷/平裝附光碟

— 英文文法・生活英語 —

用最瑣碎的時間 建立學習自信
輕鬆打下英語學習基礎！

■用心智圖概念，圖「解」複雜又難吸收的文法觀念
■30天學習進度規劃，不出國也能變身ABC
■規劃三大階段學習法，拋開制式學習，更有成效！

英文文法超圖解　　　定價 NT$ 369
ISBN：9789869528825
書系編號：文法/生活英語系列 005
書籍規格：386頁/18K/普通級/雙色印刷/平裝

說文解詩學文法　「戀」習英語寫作

精選「經典」英美情詩附中英對照，引用的詩句對應文法
概念，並且提供英語寫作範文與中譯，幫助讀者掌握寫作
起、承、轉、合的訣竅，優雅閱讀同時提升寫作功力！

學文法，戀習英語寫作　　　定價 NT$ 369
ISBN：9789869285544
書系編號：Learn Smart 062
書籍規格：304頁/18K/普通級/雙色印刷/平裝

結合英、法語字彙　享受甜點＋下午茶
語言學習的多重樂趣

精選與甜點、下午茶有關的英文字彙，皆附例句以及法語
字彙，且由專業錄音老師錄製英文單字、例句和法語單字
，學會最正統的發音！特別企劃【魔法廚房】由前輩親授
製作甜點的秘訣與心得，提供調整、創新口味的建議，幫
助店家製作出口感更符合東方人的點心，提高自家產品的
接受度與流行度！

Bon Appetit 甜點物語：英法語字彙 (附MP3)定價 NT$ 360
ISBN：9789869285582
書系編號：Learn Smart　065
書籍規格：288頁/18K/普通級/雙色印刷/平裝附光碟

國家圖書館出版品預行編目(CIP)資料

我的第一本動畫故事親子英語 / 郭玥慧著.
-- 初版. -- 臺北市：倍斯特, 2018.11　面；
公分. --（文法生活英語系列；7）
ISBN 978-986-96309-7-9（平裝附光碟）
1.英語 2.學習方法 3.親子

805.1　　　　　　　　　　　107017847

文法/生活英語 007

我的第一本動畫故事親子英語(附學習光碟MP3)

初　　版　　2018年11月
定　　價　　新台幣399元

作　　者　　郭玥慧
出　　版　　倍斯特出版事業有限公司
發 行 人　　周瑞德
電　　話　　886-2-2351-2007
傳　　真　　886-2-2351-0887
地　　址　　100 台北市中正區福州街1號10樓之2
E - m a i l　　best.books.service@gmail.com
官　　網　　www.bestbookstw.com
執行總監　　齊心瑀
執行編輯　　曾品綺
封面構成　　高鐘琪
內頁構成　　菩薩蠻數位文化有限公司
印　　製　　大亞彩色印刷製版股份有限公司

港澳地區總經銷　　泛華發行代理有限公司
地　　址　　香港新界將軍澳工業邨駿昌街7號2樓
電　　話　　852-2798-2323
傳　　真　　852-2796-5471

Simply Learning, Simply Best!

Simply Learning, Simply Best!